ACROSS THE POND

Arizona Raptors, book 2

RJ SCOTT

V.L. LOCEY

Love Lane Books

Copyright

Across the Pond (Arizona Raptors #2)

Copyright © 2019 RJ Scott, Copyright © 2019 V.L. Locey

Cover design by Meredith Russell, Edited by Sue Laybourn

Published by Love Lane Books Limited

ISBN - 9781785645068

All Rights Reserved

Dedication

We owe a huge thanks to Daniela Sarmiento who painstakingly went through this manuscript and helped us immensely in our use of Spanish in the story. All mistakes are ours… (RJ - well mine actually, as I was the one who did the final pass from her detailed notes!)
Thank you, Daniela. XXX

To my family who accepts me and all my foibles and quirks. Even the plastic banana in my holster.
VL Locey

To our small army of proofers who helped with checking the Spanish, the facts and spelling…
And, always for my family.
RJ Scott

ACROSS the POND

RJ SCOTT &
V.L. LOCEY

ONE

Alex

THERE's nothing more depressing than an empty house. The silence preyed on me when I was alone. It was an unnatural state for a guy raised with three siblings, a ton of uncles and aunts, fourteen thousand cousins spread over two countries, and a grandmother who had moved to the US a few years back to live with my parents, and who kept touch on a daily basis. The only time I'd ever had a measure of quietude as a kid had been when I'd locked myself into a closet to avoid my older brother's wrath over breaking one of his toys. Even then, within five minutes, the entire Santos-Garcia clan had arrived —including my cousin Renaldo, who worked for a locksmith—and I was sprung. My family did not believe in spending time alone.

Family was what made a person strong. *La familia hace a una persona fuerte.*

In my experience, most Latino families were tight, strong, and crazy nosy. Everyone had their noses in everyone else's business. And as much as that had driven me nuts as a teenager, now I yearned for someone to talk to. I hated how still and dead this place was. Henry was battling for his life, and Ryker had left for the All-Star game. Ryker had totally deserved to be invited, and I planned to drive out to San Luis, where my enormous family lived, and watch all the festivities. Henry *so* did not deserve what had landed on him. I had made a vow to God that if I ever got the chance, I would pound Aarni Lankinen into paste for the harm he had caused my friend.

But first, I had to pack and go visit Henry one more time. I hated to leave him. The three of us—Henry, Ryker, and I—had grown close during the season. Sharing a house will either strengthen a bond or break it. It had made us into a brotherhood of sorts. A trio of rookies bound by our love of hockey, cheesy puffs, late-night horror movies—Henry always wussed out and hid behind a pillow—and music.

Now, it was just me rattling around, washing clothes, dusting, and worrying over my friend's slow path to rejoining us. *Los tres amigos.* Sadly, I was the only friend left in this big rental house on the South side of Tucson.

"Enough. Shit, Alex, stop dwelling and get moving."

My *abuela* always said that, along with *there's no such thing as fun for the whole family*, or *my husband was a shithead*.

I missed my grandmother so much and I fingered the medallion on the end of the chain with the figure of San Sebastián engraved on it. She'd given it to me because that particular saint was the patron saint of athletes and I kept it with me tucked away where I wouldn't lose it. I didn't wear it all the time, particularly not when I was playing, but it was never far out of my reach.

San Luis was under four hours away, but some days

it felt as if she were back in Toluca with a big stupid wall between us. I longed for her hugs and a plate of her *hojarascas*. If I closed my eyes, I could taste those sweet shortbread cookies. The memories of running into her house with my siblings and cousins to grab a couple of the soft, warm treats lifted my spirits. Sometimes, she would serve them with her homemade *arroz con leche*. The rice pudding and cookie meal was special for the grandkids, and we had to promise never to let our *mamá* know she fed us sweets for dinner.

Family was a road trip away. Being there, at home, would be a blessing I desperately needed. So I got my ass in gear, tidied up the place, ran the vacuum, finished the laundry, which included the clothes I'd found in Henry's hamper, and set to serious packing. I cranked up some Bad Bunny teaming with Drake and felt some of the sadness lifting from my shoulders.

That lasted until I showed up at the rehab facility where Henry was staying, his neatly folded clothes packed in a Raptors duffel. Just parking outside this place brought me right back down, but I shoved that all aside, the rage and the melancholy, and I brought up the Alex Santos-Garcia face that everyone knew. The guy who smiled and made jokes, winked at pretty girls, and never missed confession or Sunday mass. The good boy, the son who made his *papá* proud. The fake Alejandro who everyone looked up to for being one of the few Mexican-American players in the NHL was not the real Alejandro, not by a long shot. The real Alex hid a dark, corrosive secret way deep in his soul, one that would make his parents weep and his church call him a deviant.

"*Wey*, stop," I growled to myself, turned off the

engine in my Jeep, and hauled my ass inside, where the security guard immediately stopped me.

"Hold up," he said, pushing out of his chair. I hit the brakes right inside the doors. "Let me see what's in that bag."

My gaze flew from him to the white couple whom I'd followed in, both with huge shopping bags that he'd not even blinked at.

"You didn't check their bags," I pointed out.

He was shorter than me, less muscular as well, but he had a badge and an attitude that I was oh-so familiar with. His lips flattened. "Show me the inside of that bag, *amigo*, or you can go back to wherever it was you came from."

"Right, yeah, I get it." I shoved the duffle bag at him.

He gave me a look that spoke volumes, then turned, placed the bag on the chair he'd been sitting in, and began methodically taking every damn thing out and shaking it. He shook the bag as well when it was empty, patted the insides, and ran his fingers along the seams. Throughout the fifteen-minute show, all kinds of people walked past. Doctors, nurses, aides, visitors. And there I stood, in my jeans, Raptors T-shirt, and high-tops, feeling lower than the rug we were standing on. I said nothing, something my parents had taught all of us. *"Just let them do what they feel they need to do,"* my father had explained. *"Never talk back, never give them reason to chase you, and always have your identification on you. Understand, my little ones?"*

My parents' greatest fear was being swept up in a raid and being sent back to Mexico, even though they, and now all the kids, were American citizens. My little sister and I had been born here, but my older siblings had been Dreamers until they'd passed their tests after graduating high school. Still, things being what they were, none of us in the Latino community felt one hundred percent safe…

"Fine, you can go in, but there's a time limit on visitations today. Something about fumigating for vermin. Make sure you don't get caught in it," the guard said, walking off to leave me with the tumbled mess of Henry's clothes scattered around.

I cursed under my breath.

"Cara de cerdo hijo de la gran puta!"

"Nice, I've never heard him called a pig-faced son of a bitch before." I glanced to the left to find a cute girl in a pink smock smiling up at me. Her long black hair was pulled back into a thick ponytail, her eyes were big and brown, and her lips the same color as cherry soda. "I always call him a snout-faced slug."

That made me smile a bit. "Sorry for my language."

"No harm done." She picked up and folded one of Henry's T-shirts, then handed it to me. "He's an asshole. Always give us a hard time." *Us* meaning anyone who wasn't white like he was, I was sure. I nodded. "So, Henry talks about you all the time. I see you coming in and out every day, not that I'm like stalking you or anything!"

Pink flushed her soft brown cheeks. Great. So a pretty young woman had obviously been checking me out, and I'd not picked up the signs. So typical. I was really the worst at pretending to be straight. Note to self —pay more attention to girls.

"No, no, I didn't think you were stalking me at all. I kind of saw you too," I lied like a motherfucking rug.

My eyes fell downward, to her name tag and then to her breasts, for just like a second because guys liked boobs. Hers were nice. I guessed. "Blanca, such a pretty name. My great-great-grandmother on my father's side was also a Blanca."

"Oh well, that's cool. Blanca Acosta Ramirez." She offered me her tiny hand, then sketched a cute little curtsy.

Yeah, this young woman should be making me hard, right? I mean, she wasn't of course, but she *should* be, so I needed to pretend I was interested. Fuck, I hated this so much. But she was the kind of young woman my family would love for me to date.

"Alejandro Santos-Garcia," I said, took her hand, bowed over it, and then kissed her knuckles. She giggled and batted her lashes, and before we were done folding clothes, I had her phone number. She seemed nice, a little too fangirl for me, but I could see doing dinner and a few movies with her. Maybe double-dating with some of the other guys on the team. Well, aside from Ryker, who had a boyfriend. I envied him that freedom way more than I envied his skills on the ice. I paused outside Henry's room, shook off the dour mood that wanted to return, and burst into Henry's room with a grin.

Henry was sitting up in his bed. He was still a wreck. His head and neck were bandaged to protect the eye injury he'd sustained in that car crash. He did manage a shaky smile for me despite the shattered leg in a cast that would cost him the rest of the season. God only knew what that eye injury would end up costing him. I touched the gold cross that rested on my chest, offering up a quick prayer to the Virgin Mary to keep him in her tender graces.

"Hey man, how you feeling today?" I dropped his bag onto the bed and unzipped it.

"Like I ran into a wall in a shitty sports car," he replied. I patted his hand, careful to avoid the IV embedded in his vein. "I feel like my head's packed with batting."

"You sound like my cousin Estefan after he drinks too much," I parried, carrying his clean clothes to the built-in dresser by the bathroom door. "Did you know that Tennant Rowe came here for help after his injury?" I glanced back at Henry, who had only one good eye to see me with. It was a pretty eye, the blue a rich deep color.

"My father told me that."

"Yeah, well, I think that says a lot, don't you? Look how fast he recovered! I bet by next training camp you'll be out-skating me in timed sprints." I laid his clothes into a drawer, closed it, and turned to find him staring out the window. "Hey, buddy, you hear me?"

His head swiveled in my direction. The dull look lifted, and he smiled at me.

"Alex, hey! Nice to see you," Henry called a little too loudly.

Fuck. "*Wey*, dude, good to see you!" I grinned and continued unpacking his clothes, glossing over the tics and lost words, the time spent trying to remind him of who Ryker was, and repeated questions. Head injuries were brutal; we all knew that. There wasn't a hockey player alive who wasn't aware of what concussions did to the brain. And maybe if it had just been a concussion Henry was dealing with…

"So, I met this pretty girl in the lobby," I said as I sat down. His smile seemed a little brighter, and so we talked about women and dogs until I had to leave. "I'm going home over the All-Star break, but I'll call every day, okay?"

"Sure, okay." He held up his hand for a fist bump. I rapped his knuckles gently, stuffed his dirty clothes into the duffel, and left it by the door for the laundry service to tend to while I was gone. "Bye, Alex!"

"Later, *wey*." I slipped out into the hallway, paused, closed my eyes, and took ten deep breaths. I was not going to break down here in the damn corridor. Fuck that. Crying had gotten none of us anywhere. Best to kick that shit to the curb, man up, and face the future head on. My future for a week lay in San Luis. My cell vibrated. I pulled it from my front pocket, smiled at the incoming call, and answered it immediately.

"Are you coming home soon? I went shopping at lunch. I see you in an Instagram picture. Such ratty jeans, *mijo*, and no shirt, so it seems you obviously need clothes. I found you good jeans on sale." Ugh. No, not jeans that I hadn't tried on. They'd never fit over my bubble butt and thick thighs. Jean shopping was a hands-on thing for a hockey player. Still, it was the thought that counted, right?

"*Mamá*, I have clothes."

"So you just show off your chest on purpose all over the Instagram? You don't want the kind of girl that sort of picture will draw, Alejandro. Why not share one of you in a suit? Such a handsome young man you are in a suit."

Okay, time to switch gears. "I'm leaving the rehab center now. Should be there by dinner time," I said, stalking past the guard at the door without flipping him off. My restraint was legendary.

"Good. I'm going to be leaving early and stopping at the market. Is there anything special you want?"

I flopped behind the wheel of my Jeep, the warm winds gusting around the windshield, blowing away the sadness I'd been feeling, even if just for a little while.

"Strawberry milk. Oh! Black bean dip, Limón chips... Oh! And *saladitos!* The lemon-flavored salted plums. Not the apricots. Juan likes those."

"Such a list!" She laughed. "I'll get what you like, don't worry. Your brother and sisters will be here tonight, and Dave and Mary of course. I think some of the cousins said they'd stop by, but not Héctor, because he's still mad that your *papá* wouldn't loan him a hundred dollars to buy a new cat. Imagine! We tell him the pound is filled up with cats. Go get one there, but you know Héctor. He has such grand plans. Going to breed fancy cats and sell them! *Aquel estúpido.*"

Yeah, Héctor was a stupid ass. His head was filled with flimsy get-rich-quick schemes. If only he would buckle down and work hard, he would succeed. That was a speech we'd gotten as kids daily. *Papá* would line us up before he left for work, kiss us on top of the head, and tell us that success was no accident. He would know. He'd come to America with nothing but his pregnant wife, two kids, and a dream. Now he was the manager for ten Magic Marts in the San Luis area, and my mother ran a big dental office. They'd worked their butts off. Hard work, commitment, and a dream, *Mamá* had whispered to us every night. That was all a person needed to be a successful American.

"Ignore Héctor. He's a fool. Is *Abuela* making cookies?"

"Now, what do you think?"

"Ah, I love her. And you!" I made kissy noises into the phone. "Okay, I'm leaving now. I might stop for gas and maybe a snack…"

"*¡No! Nada de snacks! Arruinarás tu apetito.*"

I sighed dramatically. "Fine, no snacks so I don't ruin my appetite."

"Good boy. Oh, and Father Delgadillo is coming as well, so make sure you shave and do not come with any trashy girl on your arm."

"*Mamá*, have I ever brought home a trashy girl?"

"Don't start now that you are playing for big-league teams. Find a nice girl, one who goes to church, and hopes to get married someday. God knows I wonder if Juan will ever settle down. I think maybe he is a gay. So you and your sister Luisa will have to find good spouses soon before I am too old to bounce a grandbaby on my knee. We'll no talk babies for Elizabeth yet."

I let my eyes drift shut. "Luisa just graduated from nursing school. Why would she want a baby so soon? And I'm in my first year on the team. You're not even fifty yet. I think you have some time left, eh? *Si Dios quiere.*"

I hurried to cross myself. God willing, she would be with us for many more years, talking about needing grandchildren and fretting over Juan, who was totally not gay at all, just loving his single life. If she only knew that she was stewing over the wrong son's sexuality.

"Such a smarty mouth. I have to go." I crossed myself again as my mother was undoubtedly doing as well. "Drive safely, *mijo.*"

"*Sí, siempre lo hago, mamá. Nos vemos ahora.*"

"*Adios*, Alejandro."

When the call ended, I sat there mulling over the

upcoming week. I was so happy to be going home, and yet there was that big dark ball of guilt and worry over my secret coming out. I'd been keeping my gayness well-hidden since college. All it had taken had been one kiss from Eddie Milkovich during a frat party to change my life forever.

For years I'd been sure that my lack of interest in girls had been due to hockey or that I was a late bloomer as my mother liked to say, even though I was well over six feet tall by the time I was fifteen. Sure, I'd dated, taken girls to dances, even made out a few times during my senior year of high school, but there had never been any real fire. Maybe, I'd reasoned, I was just one of those people who needed a commitment before I got hot and horny over a chick. Nope. It had nothing to do with a ring or hockey or my studies. I'd just never kissed another man before. Yes, I'd thought about them, picked out features on certain men that appealed to me like Chris Hemsworth's arms or Robert Pattinson's eyes, but I'd never fantasized about fucking a dude. Maybe kissing one or touching them to see if they felt different than a girl…

Looking back on it, I could see how drawn I was to men, but it took that drunken kiss behind a frat house to flip the switch. And now, three years later, that secret sat smack-dab in the middle of my chest like a boulder. Going home would, in that instance, make things so much harder. Living with Ryker had opened my eyes to how it could be, maybe, in some alternate universe where Alex Santos-Garcia wasn't a devout Catholic Mexican-American. Maybe, in that other world, Alex could find a man he loved and be open about it. Maybe in that strange upside-down land, his parents would be as cool as Ryker's parents—his stepdad/dad and his mom/stepdad—who welcomed this other Alex plus his man into their homes, hearts, and parish.

"And maybe hockey pucks will fly out of my ass," I groaned, cranked over the engine, turned up Shakira, and shoved everything down just a little deeper.

TWO

Sebastian
_____

MONEY CAN MAKE you into any kind of man you want to be.

The cash pouring into my accounts paid for this first-class seat to the US, crossing the pond from London, England, in style. Subtly attentive staff tended to my every comfort, and champagne flowed as I sat in my cozy pod in my bespoke Jasper Littman suit, Ferragamo shoes, and with my Porsche safely in Heathrow's VIP parking. I was polished, urbane, and Melanie the attendant, who told me with a soft smile and eyes full of promise she could get me *anything* I wanted, would see nothing but a successful, rich man heading to the US.

"Can I get you anything else, sir?" she asked and touched my shoulder to emphasize the question.

"Nothing, thank you."

The spark of interest in her expression was something I'd seen before. I didn't think I was particularly handsome, just well put together in my own unique way, but what I did have was the trappings of money and a confident swagger to match. The money was real, the swagger fake, but it was enough to pull whoever I wanted. If only she knew that I was more interested in Robert, the attendant who dealt with the row in front of me, then maybe she'd begin to look closer and find the clues that would give me away. Quite possibly, she'd notice that I sprawled in my seat rather than sat upright, or she'd hear vowels that weren't quite as clipped as she expected. Would she care who she found under the fake as long as I had the money to back up the image I wanted to project?

Maybe she'd like the fact that there was nothing civilized about this Brit in his expensive clothes, paying thousands for the privilege of all this luxury at the front of the plane.

"Shall I clear your things, sir?" she asked and leaned over until I got a faceful of boob, which I ignored.

I waited until the table was clear, made the appropriate amount of small talk with Melanie, carefully avoiding the aforementioned boobs, and then settled down to the matter at hand, pulling out my current notebook. I didn't work on screens. I sourced information, printed everything out, collated it, and read it as a hard copy journal. As I read, I drew up plays I could make, and only then did I commit decisions to a format others could see. My playbook on the Arizona Raptors was thick and unwieldy, and I took out the felt-tips I relied on. Green was action, blue was for further investigation, and red was for urgent attention, and I laid them next to me on the small table.

Where to start?

The Arizona Raptors. NHL team. Pretty shit by the looks of the overall stats. I ran some quick calculations in my head, going back over a few years, and it wasn't difficult to see that they were as shit as I was assuming. I didn't have to *know* hockey to see that, up until the end of the last season, they had been struggling at the very basic thing they should be doing—playing the damn game. At least this season, which was half over, they had some points on the board and were actually twenty-fourth in the league. Which was a sad thing to be pleased with, considering that was still in the bottom third.

The old management had little loyalty, the new ones were floundering in unfamiliar waters, and from the articles I'd read, most people expected the Raptors to fail. When I dug deeper, I would probably find that star performers expected constant pampering, investors were impatient, demanding quick results, and that media scrutinized and second-guessed their every move. It would be a pressure-cooker situation at the root. Then there were the three things that had fucked the team over—the change in management and ownership, the new coach, and the elephant in the room that was a criminal case against one of their big names, one Aarni Lankinen.

Other, lesser, businesses wouldn't have been able to ride out this kind of tsunami of chaos, but to give him credit, the new coach, Rowen Carmichael, had taken the bull by the horns. He'd had some tough conversations, most of which I had transcript of. Those exchanges, detailed for me to read, also gave me a basis for making an honest evaluation of every player. It would be all too easy to come to the struggling Raptors and make blanket judgments about everybody, assuming everyone was failing.

And that wasn't true. There had been some new blood this season. Three new guys who'd put up some impressive stats between them. I made a note in blue to check all three of them out and listed a whole load of questions I wanted to ask them. Looking around at some of the other teams, and how hockey worked in general, which was mostly new to me, there was an influx of new blood from something called the draft each year. The best of the best fought for NHL places, a lot of them ending up in what was called feeder teams, where they practiced until they were ready for the big teams. Then there were other newbies from colleges, and along with the draft guys and transfers up from the feeder team, there was a whole group of younger guys.

Jason had emailed an information sheet on each player, and I worked my way through them, sliding the biggest arsehole known to man, Aarni Lankinen, to the bottom of the pile because, last I'd heard, he was heading for prison.

Ryker Madsen was first on the list, the brightest star. He was all Instagram'd up, Twitter as well, and had a healthy following because of someone called Tennant Rowe? Seemed like Tennant was a big thing, and I added that to my list for further investigation. Ryker was a pretty boy, all sharp edges and curly hair, and his smile was infectious. The mean and moody team shots were all spoiled by that smile, which hinted at someone who was comfortable in their own skin. He was the flashy goal-scoring type, and he was the perfect poster boy for the Raptors. If we could get more people following him, loving him, then we'd have a whole new audience to pick through. But he was just a little too perfect, well, apart from the gay thing, which appeared to be causing some issues.

Henry Greenaway, he'd been one of the new ones, but he was out for the rest of the season with a head injury. Looking at the situation cynically, which always made me feel dirty, I could build a campaign about his recovery, but I'd seen abusive relationships for myself, and the last thing the kid needed was to have cameras in his face the entire time.

Cameras? Oh, interesting, I should make a note about that.

A documentary, behind the scenes, that kind of thing, showing a happy, united team who pranked each other and weren't all old-school assholes.

"Can I get you something, sir?" I looked up to see Robert, not Melanie, checking me out. "Or is there anything I can help you with?"

"Is Melanie on a break?" I asked and deliberately dropped my gaze to crotch level, which wasn't hard, considering Robert was *right there*.

"Yes, sir," Robert replied and raised a single eyebrow. Much as he fitted my type, short, slim, blue eyes, short blond hair, tending toward the effeminate, I was head deep in research, and rich guys did not take flight attendants into cramped plane bathrooms to get blow jobs.

"Not at the moment," I hedged.

He pouted, then winked at me. "Come find me if you need anything."

I watched him sashay away, wondering if just for a moment I could let the veneer of responsible-businessman-me fade away and pull out the old Seb, who would demand Robert get on his knees right the hell now. The feeling passed, and even though my cock disapproved of my decision, my brain was right back on the issue in hand.

Which was when I turned the page and saw *him*. With a waning erection and thoughts of nasty bathroom sex in my head, I went straight to the details of one Alejandro Ricardo Santos-Garcia, or Alex, as he was known to his friends.

Fuck me. Alex was a long way past young and malleable for my purposes, and right onto sexy, fuckable, and fitting into all kinds of other thoughts I'd had.

I turned back to Henry's page and then flicked to Alex, just to see if the visceral reaction I'd had was a fluke.

It wasn't.

I like blue eyes. But Alex had deep brown eyes, so dark that I couldn't make out the pupil in this team shot. With dark hair and a rangy figure, he was the very opposite of the blond thing I had going on with Robert the alternate attendant. Add in that Alex was taller than my five ten and that his sharp focus was intimidating, and it hit me that maybe I'd been fucking the wrong guys my entire life.

Alex had Instagram, and I was driven to see more photos of this sexy hockey player, but his posts were mostly of food and one of him at the beach with friends. One of him with his rugged good looks to his warm sun-kissed skin to the dinners he shared with Spanish-sounding names. I couldn't talk the talk, sucked at most languages, but for him, I could learn the words for all manner of sexual requests.

Down, boy. This is a job. We do not fuck the hired help. We are above that.

I flicked past Alex's page, after making a note that he had the potential to be the poster boy for the Raptors. After burying myself in the profiles of the rest of the team, there was no one who stood out to me, not in the same way Alex did. So I checked him out on Wikipedia to start with the dry facts.

He'd been drafted in the third round, which was apparently an okay thing, then spent four years playing collegiate hockey at Arizona State University. He came from a big, extended family from a town not far from the Arizona Raptors arena. He had two sisters, one older and one younger, and an older brother, and clicking on a few links revealed his dad managed ten of something called Magic Mart, in the San Luis area. Alex was a Mexican-American and a practicing Catholic. Good clean boy with no history of anger issues or wild parties or sleeping around or getting girls pregnant. In fact, there was no hint of scandal attached to him or his hardworking family. I widened the search and found a couple of hockey forums that mentioned his name. I read comments about his stats, his performance on ice, his position, on joining the Raptors.

What I didn't expect to see was the animosity thrown at him. The racial slurs, the threats that he should be sent home, and worst, the terrorization against anyone connected to him. That would have to be handled if I thought that Alex was the best person to make the face of the team.

I couldn't understand the strength of the vitriol, though. Being a Brit didn't make me immune to seeing racial tension. As a nation, we were very good at forming groups and excluding others. But these were *genuine* fans of the *actual* Raptors calling out the young man who might well be one of the saviors of their shitty team. None of it computed.

"Sir, we're coming in to land at Tucson International shortly." Melanie nodded at the papers and electrical items spread around me. I packed it all away, closing down the iPad, storing my journal, and staring out the window at the night sky. Tucson was right there, just on the horizon, a brilliantly lit city in the middle of what I knew was a desert. I could see the faint shape of mountains, but it was too dark to make out most of what we were passing over.

Getting through customs at LaGuardia had been time-consuming, but I'd not been able to secure a direct flight to Tucson. Although on the plus side, that delay in New York sped things up when I arrived in Arizona a great deal, but I still had a small wait at baggage claims, and then it was a waiting game.

"Seb! Seb!" I turned to see my friend, Jason Westman-Reid, part-owner of the Raptors, jogging toward me, reaching me, and pulling me into a close hug. "So good to see you, man," he said.

"And you," I answered truthfully. I'd formed a close friendship with the loud, somewhat annoying American in my first year at Cambridge, and it hadn't waned all through business school. He'd decided to come to the UK to study to get away from his overbearing dad, and that had been my luck because he was more or less instantly my best friend. Now, with an ocean between us, we emailed, kept in touch through Facebook every so often, and exchanged Christmas cards. I'd sympathized when his dad died, sent flowers, but it took a personal cry for help to get me stateside. My work was in the UK, but I owed Jason big-time, and if I could clear my debt with this one thing, just three months, then I was happy to do it.

"Are you sure you're okay in the pool house?" he asked, among chatter about his family, kids, Lewis and Deborah, and his wife, Yvonne, all of whom were his entire life.

He'd never struck me as the type to settle down, not after I'd spent a lot of time shadowing his whoring days at Cambridge, but somehow he'd found it all. Not that I envied him. We were in our early thirties, and I had a lot more living to do before finding that mythical *one*. Even then, I wasn't sure that was even possible for me. My mum had thought she'd found the *one*, but he'd left her as soon as she'd announced she was pregnant. Not that we needed him. We'd done okay, the two of us, fought and worked hard, and when I'd bought her and my aunt Olivia a new house in the quiet countryside a few years back, we'd come full circle. She'd looked after me, and now it was my turn to care for her.

"The pool house? Of course I am. I've seen the photos, and it's bigger than a hotel room."

As soon as we left the airport, I launched into questions about the Raptors, and Jason seemed primed and ready to answer. He was going to be my link to the team, the intermediary to help me understand what was happening there.

"Tell me about the Aarni situation." I began by addressing the shitshow that had just occurred.

"Bought out, sentenced, gone, thank fuck."

"Which leaves a hole on the team, I presume?"

"Yeah, particularly with Henry out as well, but I think Rowen and Cam have it in hand."

Rowen being the coach, Cam, Jason's brother.

"And the money situation?" I prompted when we slipped into silence.

Jason shot me a quick look, then focused back on the road ahead. "We can pay you," he defended.

I thumped his arm as he pulled away from a set of lights. "I owe you. This is free of charge. Call it a holiday of sorts."

"A vacation? This is one hell of a vacation, but thank you for coming over."

I shrugged as if it meant nothing when actually having Jason ask me to help meant everything. Being valued was the best part of the man I'd made myself into. "I'm looking forward to the challenge. I was between contracts." That last bit was a lie, but I didn't want anyone to know I'd spent an entire week rearranging contracts and delaying projects so I could come to the US. There was no way I was letting Jason know that because he had enough worries to be going on with, and my evasion must have worked, as he sent me a grateful smile.

"Where do you want to start? Because if I know you, I won't be able to persuade you to leave off starting this until the morning."

"I'd like to see the arena, get a sense of it, and also meet Coach Carmichael, hit the ground running, so to speak."

Jason pressed a button on the steering wheel and connected to COACH, which appeared on his display.

"What now, Jason?" A voice echoed loudly in the car. "I thought we did all the talking and the arguing already today."

Jason rolled his eyes, "Fucks sake, Mark, why are you answering Rowen's phone?"

"Because Rowen is in the shower after we just spent all afternoon in bed and——"

"I'm in the car," Jason interrupted. "With Seb," he added forcefully.

"Oh, so no more embarrassing talk about sexing up my boyfriend, then," Mark deadpanned.

"Jeez, no."

Mark was the youngest of the Westman-Reid brothers, as far as I recalled. The black sheep, the one who'd fueled many a drunken, regretful discussion with Jason back in the day. He'd never forgiven himself for not standing up to his asshole dad and losing touch with Mark. Clearly, bridges had been mended, and everything was back on an even keel now.

"Hi, Mark," I said by way of introduction. "I know we haven't met yet, but I'm here to work with the team."

"Oh, I know. Hi, Seb. Jason has told us a lot about you."

"Not all good things, I hope," I quipped, and Mark and I shared a laugh. *Keep it light; keep it easy. People like me more when I am amusing Seb.*

"No, it's mostly good," Mark said. "You want me to get Rowen to call you?"

"Could you meet us at the rink in an hour?" Jason asked and side-eyed me for my approval, to which I nodded. I expected there to be negotiation from Mark, but he said they'd be there, and suddenly it was all looking very real.

AT THE RINK, Rowen—call me Coach—Carmichael sized me up in a few seconds. "Not too much hockey experience, then?" he asked after we'd exchanged names. Jason and Mark watched from a distance, allowing this meeting to go largely unwitnessed.

"Business is business," I replied cryptically. "A team is the same as a company when you get down to brass tacks."

He frowned at me, "Hockey is a different kind of world."

"I respectfully disagree. It's the same as going into any company for me to assess and then tell it like it is." He opened his mouth as if he was going to disagree, and I held up a hand to stop him. "At the end of the day, the only way to change people in any kind of organization is to tell them in the clearest possible terms what they're doing wrong. And if the members of any team, sports or business, or anything else that has a structure, if they don't want to listen, they don't belong on the team," I said, and even though Rowen finally nodded, I could see he bristled a little.

"One question. Are you telling me in that perfectly structured statement delivered in your very British voice, that what I'm doing with the Raptors is wrong?" He crossed his arms over his chest, and I didn't have to be an expert in body language to understand his defensiveness and outward show of no respect.

"No," I reassured at speed. "What you are doing is perfectly right. I'm here to work alongside you, not touching the team or the playing but working on the way people perceive the Raptors and you, particularly in light of what happened with one of your players."

He "hmmm'd" at me, in that way people did when they weren't wholly buying into everything, so I added the killer line.

"You were called in to turn this team around, and

you utilized rule one. You made it clear from day one that you're in charge and imposed your leadership rather than waiting to earn it. I admire that. What I want to do is assist you in building a culture of success in the larger team, the staff, the media, the way the team's fans interact."

I couldn't help but think of Alex at that point and some of the abuse he was getting from his own team's fans. That had to be the first thing to go, and what I needed to do was set goals and hit them.

Coach Rowen held out his hand, and we shook again, firmly, the bargain struck.

And so it began.

THREE

Alex
_____

COMING BACK to the ice after a week away had been a shock to the system, and not all in a bad way. I'd been spoiled and pampered at home, fed like a king, and coddled by my mother, grandmother and little sister, Elizabeth, who was thrilled to have another child in the house to take some of the attention from her. Her *quinceañera* was in three months, and she was feeling the pressure big-time.

I'd spent hours hanging out with my high school buddies, playing basketball, going to the movies, cruising the streets of San Luis in my cousin Elonso's 1965 Chevy Impala Super Sport. He was a member of the San Luis Lowrider Motor Club, and his purple Impala drew a ton of attention. Elonso never seemed to be lacking a sexy lady at his side on Friday nights when the club met, and he was generous in making sure I had a companion as well. I did my best to fit in, draping my arm around the young woman plastered to my side, tossing out ribald jokes to ensure I was as straight as a gay guy could be. It sucked, but I did it because… well, because I was too scared not to.

Leaving behind the strict masculine structure of a Latin neighborhood felt good. I'd spent a good amount of time among my cousins and school friends, and while many of them were accepting of the LGBT community, a lot were not even close to being allies. Add in the mixed signals from the Catholic Church where being gay or lesbian is supposedly okay, but if you act on your drives, then it's sinful—compounding, the burden of being accepted. Quite a few Latinx came out in their English world but hid it from the Hispanic world and church. I'd not even worked up the courage to come out in my English world. But, and this was key, the more time I spent with Ryker, the more I longed to live my life open and free.

Seeing him bound back into the dressing room was as if someone had lit a beacon.

"No shit, look at the superstar. You rocked that All-Star shit, man," Colorado said, striding over to greet Ryker at the door. They clapped each other on the back, Ryker's grin infectious. I walked over and got a brisk hug.

"Man, that was some crazy time. Dude, I got to play with so many greats. They were so cool!" Ryker gushed as more and more of the team gathered around him.

"You looked good out there. Focused, in control." Colorado clapped him on the shoulder and then ambled off to find an empty bathroom and sing. Yeah, the dude sang before every game. Said it helped him zone in. Whatever worked for him. We were all used to goalie eccentricities. Some tenders talked to their pipes, some caressed them, some carried water from Canada to the rink and sprinkled it on the blue ice under their skates, some whispered prayers to Nordic gods. Our netminder belted out heavy metal songs in the men's room. And woe betide anyone who happened to need to piss or shit and interrupted the concert. Poor Henry had made that mistake only once and had been ejected from the bathroom by an irate goalie waving a fat stick over his head. Colorado was cool, obviously, being a metal musician and just in general, but he had a short temper.

"Come on, sit down and tell me all about it," I said, latching onto my roommate and hauling him to our cubicles.

"Oh my God, it was great. I'll fill you in when we get home, okay? How's Henry?" Ryker asked as he shrugged out of his suit jacket.

I'd been here for a while, had played some soccer with Brennan, and Vlad. The big Russian defenseman had become our captain before the season had started, and he was fitting into his role well. He had this easygoing way about him off the ice, and his English was smooth as icy vodka, with just a subtle flavoring of Russian. Two older guys had the alternate captain letters. None of us rookies yet, but that was to be expected. You had to earn those letters. That was one of my goals, to get an A on my sweater within two seasons and maybe someday fly with Ryker to the All-Star game. Man, my parents would be so proud…

"He's okay, you know, considering. I think maybe he's just really down." I slid my foot into my sock and pulled it up over my shin guards. "His folks are all worried that he's not working hard enough, so they keep pushing him, but I'm not sure that's the way to go about it. You think we should talk to him, maybe? See if he's depressed?"

Ryker sighed as he hung up his jacket. "How can he *not* be depressed? Between the mental shit Aarni had put him through, then the accident, and now not knowing if he'll ever play again…"

"He will. He'll play again." I made the sign of the cross.

"I don't know, man. Eye injuries are some serious shit. There's a guy who played with my dad, took a slap shot to the eye. He had all kinds of major problems, like a retinal tear. He came back, sure, after forever, but his vision was never the same, and his play suffered. He finally retired two years after the injury."

"Fuck," I whispered.

"Yeah, it's not an easy road." Ryker dropped down beside me on the bench, his shirt now hanging behind him with his jacket. "I don't want to blow smoke up his ass, but I don't want to not encourage him. Maybe we should talk with his family?"

"Yeah, well, I did, and they had this weird mindset that enough hard work would lift his spirits right up. Totally Midwestern, you know? Like they still think mental illness is something to be ashamed of. I think we should talk to Henry, feel him out, see if we can pick up something."

"Okay, yeah, we can do that."

I nodded. "It's good to have you back. Penn is cool and all. but he's like"—I shrugged as I dressed my other leg—""… he's got this whole vibe like he's laid back, but we all know he's about as laid back as a rattlesnake. *Cierras los ojos y blam!*" I slapped my hands together.

Ryker gave me that look that said, "translation needed please." "You close your eyes and *blam*!"

"Yeah, snake bit. That kind of does describe him. I bet one of those tats of his is of this huge gnarly rattlesnake, fangs all bared and dripping venom."

"He *does* have one of a snake, curled up and shaking its rattle right above his ass," I said, then chuckled. Ryker lifted an eyebrow. Then I caught what I'd said. "Not that I've been checking out his ass or anything."

"No, of course not." He smiled, patted my face, and stood. There was a lot in that reply that sat funny on my shoulders, but game time was quickly approaching, so I let it go.

We hit the ice an hour later to face off against Edmonton, which would be game one in a back-to-back, which had us rushing to Canada bright and early in the morning. After that game, we'd make a short Canadian road trip, then be back in Tucson in just under a week. Ryker was keyed up for this game as we were facing the backup goalie for the Oilers, Benoit Morin, a guy he'd played with up at Owatonna University.

The first ten minutes of the game were pretty uneventful. Ryker and I were clicking well, but we had a new guy at left wing. Coach had moved the lines around to accommodate the loss of Aarni and Henry. A big D-man had been called up from the feeder team to replace Lankinen, and we had gotten Jens Hauger from the fourth line, and a new guy from the minors had taken his place. It didn't help that both teams were groggy and rusty from the week-long break, so the play was spotty.

Ryker had gotten a weak shot in on Morin, which the lanky tendie had deflected with ease. Jens found his stride with about five minutes left in the period. We'd been stuck in the neutral zone, trying to get out when Jens, a short Norwegian with the heart of a lion, picked up a giveaway. With Ryker and me coming to back him up, the quick little winger moved in on Morin and took a snappy shot that Jens over the goalie's left shoulder and into the net.

Javan threw his hands into the air as the red light flashed, and the fans got to their feet. Ryker and I got to him first, the D-men piling into the group hug in the corner. Now that we were up by a goal, things felt a little less fractured. During the break, Coach talked us up, pointing out that we'd now cracked Morin's armor a bit.

Behind him stood the associate coaches as well as a well-dressed man with short brown hair and light brown eyes. Fashionably scruffy, which was superhot, he was scribbling in a paper notebook, his gaze flickering up every now and then. He was pretty in an elite sort of way, and he held my eye. When our gazes met, I felt it, right between my pecs, where you'd feel the first pangs of heartburn. Only this sensation was nothing like the burn of too many jalapeño poppers. No, this was different. It made the fine hairs on my sodden neck bristle with awareness. I wet my lips. His mouth curled up into a soft smile that set fire to my skin. I averted my gaze quickly before someone saw me checking out the man in the sharp gray suit.

"Get the puck elevated and up. You're never going to get anything by that kid, shooting at his chest. Every point counts now. Don't let the trash talk online get into your head. People are always going to be tossing shit at us, some of it is well deserved, but some of it isn't. Management is working to fix that issue, so when you see this fellow lurking around, don't think anything of it.

Sebastian is here to help us improve our social networking online media presence. Is that the proper terminology?"

"Close enough to count," Sebastian said, then smiled fully. It lit up his face in ways I shouldn't have noticed but couldn't help not to. And that accent was super attractive.

"Well, tweeting isn't my thing. I come from the old days when folks were all agog about a cordless phone," Coach joked, the team chuckled, and I stared at the sexy older Brit, unable to look away until someone slapped the back of my head. Jens nudged me in the side, his smile as big as his hazel eyes. "Sebastian will probably be touching base with all of you to go over whatever it is he's going to go over. Make yourself available to him, that is a request from the owners, and tighten up your corner work."

With that, the suits left, leaving us stinky sweaty ones to rehydrate and rest for ten more minutes. I thought of checking my phone to see if the team had made any kind of official announcement about Sebastian with the sexy scruff, but phones weren't allowed during game time under penalty of death or bag skates. So I sat there, sucking down lemon-flavored electrolyte replacer while listening to Ryker and Jens talk about a trip to Norway during the summer, while I daydreamed of older British men.

"You'll come, right?" Ryker asked, jarring me from the haze of lust that I'd tumbled into.

"Oh, uhm, I don't know. I've never traveled outside the country except to visit family in Mexico. Maybe?"

"You'd love Norway! It's beautiful, friendly, and the women are so pretty," Jens boasted. "Oh, well, I forget,

Ryker…" He paused to parse Norwegian into English. "You're gay with a boyfriend. Bring him! Norwegians are so very accepting. We have a big house outside Oslo, and my mother loves company. She'll feed you so well you'll bust a gut!"

"Well, I'm bi, but sure, I'd love to travel with Jacob over the summer. I'll for sure bring it up."

They both looked at me.

"Yeah, awesome, pretty Norwegian girls." I hoped that sounded more enthusiastic to them than it had to me. "Love me some blondes with big boobs."

That announcement got a round of agreement from just about everyone in the Raptors dressing room, even Ryker couldn't argue. I stared at my skates for the rest of the break, wondering how Ry had ever found the nerve to be so upfront about his sexuality. I mean, saying it to the team like that had taken balls. And no one had said anything bad back. Lifting my gaze from my feet, I swept the room, wondering if maybe someday they'd all be as accepting of a gay man among them as they were of a bisexual man.

Hockey time swiped away the worries of locker room politics. Edmonton woke up in the second and tied the game, sneaking one past Colorado that he should have had. He knew it. He worked his crease with his skates with a fury, dropping down low into a butterfly stance, his gaze manic inside his mask after that goal against us.

We ended up going into overtime tied 1-1, with a flip-flop rebound goal off an Edmonton boot that rolled between Morin's legs. The puck wobbled, then fell to its side in exhaustion just over the line. I knew how that puck felt. All I'd wanted was to go home and crash, but

Ryker was determined to meet up with his buddy Benoit at a local watering hole called The Crimson Cactus. It was the Raptors' hangout, just a block from the barn, and no way in hell was Madsen taking my whiny no for an answer.

"Fine, sweet Jesus, I'll meet you there." I shoved at Ryker playfully as Colorado waited by the door, wearing his usual black suit, white shirt, skinny black-and-white skull tie ensemble.

"Don't back out, Alex," Ryker warned, then jogged off to leave with our goalie. I'd been hanging back in hopes of… well, it didn't matter. Stupid anyway to want to get another look at that Sebastian guy. He was probably married with kids. As I slid my arm into the jacket of my suit, my phone buzzed. I leaped on it, surprised to see a call from my little sister, Elizabeth, or Bitty, as we all called her.

"Hey, little bitty one," I said, holding the phone to my ear with my shoulder as I yanked a comb through my wet hair. "Did you sprain your thumbs?"

"Oh. My. God. Alex, I swear I am going to cancel my *quinceañera* if they don't stop!"

"*Respira profundo, hermanita,*" I teased and winced when my comb snagged on a knot.

"Don't tell me to take deep breaths! Alex, please be my *chambelán de honor*. Please. *Mamá* and *Abuela* are making me crazy with the lists of boys they think are suitable."

I snickered softly, pulled a wild lock of hair down into place, and tossed my comb onto the shelf next to my aftershave and a new razor.

"Then pick someone you like," I said, shoving my tie into my pocket and grabbing my personals bag.

"Surely, the list of boys you're crushing on must be long."

"Okay, you stop with your shit right now! You know there's no list. And if there was, how the hell would I walk up to someone as cute as Lorenzo Milano and ask him?"

I opened my mouth to reply, then snapped it shut. Who was I to give her advice on how to ask someone she liked to be her escort on such a special day? I wasn't brave enough to even ask another man out to coffee. I pushed through the exit, giving the security man dawdling by the players' entrance a nod.

"Alex, are you there?" Elizabeth asked.

"Yeah, I'm here. Listen, Bitty, I know how overwhelming the family is at times, but try not to let them run your life for you. If you want to ask Lorenzo, then ask him, but don't let *Mamá* or *Abuela* or *Tía* Luisa, Sofía, Magdalena, or any of the other women bully you."

"Ayeeeeeeee, I know that, Alejandro! Tell me *how* to ask Lorenzo."

I had no answer for my baby sister, not a truthful one anyway. I paused just outside the door, my gaze landing on Sebastian jogging toward me, a smile on his lips and the hot desert wind in his hair.

"Alejandro, oh my *God*, why are you so stupid tonight?" She then called me several bad names in Spanish, then hung up after informing me that she was calling Luisa because older sisters were way smarter than older brothers.

With nothing to do but talk to him, I slid my phone into my pocket and met him head on.

"I didn't catch you at a bad time, did I?" he asked. I

shook my head. "Good, I was hoping we could talk a bit, if you're free?"

"I was going to go meet the guys for a beer, but uhm…" I waved at the sky because I was stupid—just ask my baby sister—and the sky was obviously where hockey players went for beer.

"So is that a no?"

God, he was sexy and foreign and whiskery. Not over whiskery, just the right amount to rub on my belly or inside my thighs or scrub along my balls. Shit.

"No, it's not a no."

Santa María, Madre de Dios ayúdame.

Was it a sacrilege to ask the Virgin Mary to help you fight off dirty gay thoughts about some man you barely knew? Probably. I was so going to Hell…

FOUR

Seb

FINISHING that last page of notes had left me walking through empty hallways and past a surprised guard who eyed me with suspicion until I flashed my pass at him. I read his badge and saw his name was Lewis. "Oh yeah, I know about you," he said

I held out my hand, "Seb."

"You're the Brit that's come to fix the team. Not that it needs fixing."

Well, that was a loaded statement. "Okay."

Lewis drew back his shoulders and lifted his chin. "Not sure why they couldn't use a real American anyways."

Really? He was going *there*? I'd worked with some of the biggest companies in the world, most of them outside of London, and he was worrying about me not being American? "If it helps, my great-grandmother on my dad's side was originally from New York." I could lie with the best of them, given Granny J was from Liverpool, was still with us at a hundred and two, and to my knowledge had never left England. She was the old-fashioned type who believed that a day out at the beach in the rain was an exotic adventure, and was as wary of Americans as it seemed Lewis was about Brits. They'd be a fine pair squaring off in the hallway, although knowing Granny J, she'd probably take down the tattooed behemoth blocking the exit.

He eyed me closely. "New York, you say?"

"Yes, so that makes me an honorary American, don't you agree?"

He looked confused for a moment. Then something inside must have connected. "Sure, I guess it does." Then he sniffed and crossed his beefy arms over his chest. "We don't want foreigners taking our jobs, can't even get a decent white American team together here. And I don't mean the Canadians, I mean, most of those are okay I guess."

Wow, he was defensive, to the point of belligerence. Was this the first thing that players saw when they entered the Arena? I made a mental note to look into this more deeply. Maybe the values that needed massaging were more entrenched than I'd thought.

"Does Arizona have a lot of *foreigners* taking jobs, then?" I asked and smiled so hard I thought my face would crack. I could play this game, act as if it was just banter, collect all the information I could. I could thank Hugh Grant for making us Brits look like bumbling fools and therefore completely innocent of any wrongdoing or underhand dealings of any sort.

"All the time." Lewis shook his head, "I was lucky to get this job at all."

"How terrible," I agreed, and Lewis regarded me warily, making me think my sarcasm mask had slipped too far.

Soon enough, the entire team, including security, admin, and whoever else I would be adding to my company plan would all know me. When I went deep into any kind of company, I learned everything from the ground up. I'd talk to cleaners, security personnel, highfliers, middle management, the scared employees who didn't really want to talk, and the ones who didn't give a shit about the company. I rooted everything out until I got a clear picture of how things worked, and non-American or not, I was bloody good at what I did.

But for now, I would introduce myself to everyone who wondered why a stranger was poking his nose into every room he found, start spreading my name.

"Nice to meet you too, Lewis. Have you worked here long?"

He looked around himself as if he was concerned others would be watching. That reaction right there gave me insight into more than just one guard at an exit. He was wary, frowning, and likely had a million thoughts spinning in his head about how what he said could come back and bite him. All that from a simple question about how long he had been there.

"Six years this Christmas," he offered, and that was clearly all I was going to get.

"You must have seen a lot," I said and saw the instant he shut down. I'd been labeled as dangerous to his well-being, and I could see that he was loyal, which was a good thing, but scared, which was a bad thing. I'd been led to believe that the Westman-Reid family had taken the time to start building relationships, but it appeared that hadn't trickled down to the security staff yet. I made a mental note to follow that up.

"Anyway, really good to meet you. Hope to speak

soon." I shook his hand again and left the building, with all kinds of theories beginning to form about the Raptors.

Then I saw *him.*

Spotting Alex, just standing there all on his own talking on his phone, I thanked the stars that I'd delayed leaving the rink, then got caught up talking to Lewis. Asking him to talk wasn't what I'd meant to say. Hell, I don't know what I meant to say. Maybe my lizard-brain just wanted to stand near him and stare. Maybe the sensible side of me saw this as a moment to connect with the young player one-on-one. Who knew?

All that concerned me right now was getting some face time with the player, and I waited for him to give out his excuses and finally agree to go with me.

"Can we find somewhere quiet to talk?" I asked after he'd pointed at the sky and explained he was meeting hockey players for a drink.

He was flustered, eyes wide, and I think it was obvious I unnerved him. Was that a good thing? I'm not sure I wanted him looking quite so much like a frightened rabbit. I needed him onside if I was going to make him the face of the Raptors.

"Quiet," he repeated and waved to his left, "there's a coffee place I sometimes go to."

"Okay, sounds good." I watched him turn to leave and then immediately turn to face me again.

"Just let me…" He shrugged his bag and gestured with it. He liked using his hands to express himself, and I was intrigued. I followed him to a dusty Jeep. When he'd locked up and pocketed the keys, we resumed our walk, and while we were busy negotiating the crosswalk, we didn't talk. It was only when we were at the counter waiting for a Frappuccino, him, and a flat white, me, did he begin to talk.

"I bet it's weird being inside a coffee shop," he said.

"Weird how?"

"Well, over here, we have shops that just sell coffee and have sofas to sit on, and things must be odd for you."

I cleared my throat. "We do have coffee shops in England as well."

His eyes widened again, and he appeared to be half-confused, half-embarrassed. "Oh," was all he managed.

"And electricity," I added because I couldn't resist the way he was reacting, all flustered and way too cute for me to ignore. This could go two ways; he could get so embarrassed that this meeting would be for nothing, or he could take control of himself and react with humor.

He side-eyed me, then dimpled a smile, which went straight toward my libido crashing hard and stealing my breath.

"Electricity?" He deliberately widened his eyes and rounded his mouth in shock. "Like for reals?" He blinked at me, and my libido went from spinning at the dimples to sitting up and taking notice.

"And inside bathrooms," I added and grinned at him.

Laughter reached his eyes, and I knew I'd won him over.

"Next thing you'll tell me is you don't all know the Queen."

I shrugged. "Nah, we all know the Queen."

Our conversation was interrupted by his name being called, and we picked up our drinks from the end counter. We'd almost made it away and to a table when Alex was stopped by a family of four.

"Big fan," the dad said, pumping Alex's hand so hard I wondered if Alex would shake him off.

He didn't. He stood and listened as the dad, followed by the equally hockey-mad kids, began talking stats and records. I let it work its way out, watched Alex engage the crowd. There was nothing in his expression that screamed he was nervous, not one ounce of caution. He gave everything of himself, talking about his plans, Ryker, the Stanley Cup, the season, and giving a sigh when the dad commiserated about Lankinen being an asshole.

Of course, the dad using the word asshole caused the mom to lose her cool and hiss that the kids were listening, so Alex didn't get to answer, which was a good thing. Instead, he signed a couple of things, a menu and a receipt, and crouched to talk to the girl and boy who were no more than ten and hung on to his every word. There was an approachability to Alex, and I instinctively knew I'd picked the right person for my plans. All I needed to do now was convince Alex he wanted to be part of them.

He chose a table at the back and around a corner, probably to give us time to talk without his being recognized, but I chose to think he wanted me to himself. Because that is the kind of idiot I am.

"You don't mind it when people talk to you like that?"

He sipped his drink and smiled at me over the rim of his cup. "It's weird, but it's the job, one of the nicest parts actually, up there with playing for an NHL team. Not that I ever dreamed about being recognized, not as much as I dreamed about playing in the big leagues. No one really wants to get noticed, I guess." He stopped talking, and the smile had gone, vanished as he repeated what he'd said with the extra provisos, falling out of him as if he was using words as his thought process. We'd have to work on that if he was to be the team ambassador, but on a personal level, I thought it was endearing. And hot.

"What are your thoughts on Aarni Lankinen?" I asked and sat back in my chair, nursing my coffee. I would be asking the same question of everyone, working out which of the players still had their heads stuck in the past.

"Henry is one of my best friends." He placed his drink on the table and leaned forward. There was so much raw emotion in his expression, along with the same determined focus that I'd seen in footage of him when he was on the ice. "He's in a hospital with a head injury, and the man who nearly killed him is going to jail. I'm glad for it." I didn't need to use my talent for reading people to see the anger in Alex, and the tone he used was one that implied he wouldn't be arguing the situation.

"Would you have said that to the dad of the family if he hadn't been interrupted?"

The question hung between us for a single moment, and then he let out a noisy sigh.

"No. I would have changed the subject myself because my opinion isn't something that needs to be aired to the world. I have enough to deal with normally, let alone tripping myself up and getting into a discussion about how good or bad Aarni was for the team. I just want to play hockey, and I want my friend Henry back on the ice, and I hate Aarni for what he did. The first thing? The hockey? That is in the public domain. The rest, that is all me. Private me. But sometimes when things get too much, God, I want to shout."

That was a double-edged answer. I liked how he said he would change the subject, that he would show restraint, but also the passion in his eyes for what he really thought was an emotional charge that he would have to restrain.

Was I even right to ask him to hold things back?

Why am I even worrying about it? I need to do what's best for the team.

"So I wanted to talk to you because I'm here to work on the negative way the public may perceive the Raptors."

He let out a humorless laugh. "And the rest of the league."

"Them as well." I leaned forward to mirror his position and ignored my coffee. Time for the first approach to someone who was likely going to be reluctant to any and all ideas that meant he could be the poster boy for the Raptors. "Revenue is falling, you know that, and the online vitriol has only ramped up with the Aarni situation." Alex winced at the use of Lankinen's name. "One of the ways we'd like to approach this is to focus on the new blood in the team, talk up the positive future."

"You mean Ryker," he said and smiled. "He's an amazing player and has the whole backstory going for him."

I decided that honesty was the best policy and hoped that Alex didn't think he was second best. "Ryker seemed like a good choice on the surface, but he's openly bisexual, and that won't sit well with our demographic as the face of our team."

All the blood left Alex's face. He went so pale I thought he was going to pass out, and then he covered what had to be disbelief by picking up his drink and hiding. He did know that about Ryker, right? Everyone knew. It wasn't a secret, and Ryker's father had married another hockey player, so it was open knowledge. So why did Alex look so shocked? Did he disapprove? Was he sickened? It turned out that him thinking he was second best was the least of my worries.

"What's wrong?" I asked, and he closed his eyes briefly.

"Wrong? What's wrong is that just because Ryker doesn't fit in the lines you've drawn, that he's cast aside as if he doesn't mean anything."

"No, wait—"

"*Pinche pendejo*. He's the best player we have, and without him, the Raptors have no chance at winning shit."

"That isn't entirely true. They have you—"

"Me? I'm the kid from the wrong end of hockey town! Every time I go out on the ice, I hear slurs," he said through gritted teeth.

"We could manage that—"

"Some of the words thrown at me you wouldn't even picture in your head, let alone throw them at a player. And this isn't just from the fans, but other teams as well, from the agitators who want me to fuck up." He wasn't letting me talk, and he pushed his drink to one side and leaned even closer to me. "My skin is darker, I speak two languages, my family is everything to me, and my heritage is from over the border, but that doesn't define my hockey-playing skills, even though some people think it should." He stood so fast his chair hit the wall behind him, but he wasn't shouting. If anything, his tone was icy cold. "You know and I know that Ryker is the best on this team, and who he loves has nothing to do with his skills. So you can take that eighties homophobic shit you're shoveling and shove it where the sun don't shine."

He stalked away from the table, and for a few moments, I was shocked immobile, processing what I'd said, what he said and, more importantly, what he thought. Then I hurried after him, vaulting a chair and reaching the door just as it shut in my face. I yanked it open and jogged to catch him up, but he had a rare head of steam on him, and his stride was longer than mine. Only just before we reached the bar he was heading to did I finally manage to get in front of him, then held a hand to his chest to stop him.

He had murder in his eyes, a temper so high the color had flooded back into his face and left his cheeks scarlet.

"Get. Out. Of. My. Way." He bit out each word and attempted to sidestep me, but if there was one thing I'd learned in life, it was how to be the best obstacle ever. In a smooth move, I guided him back into a small space between the bar and the chicken restaurant next door.

"Let me explain," I began.

"There's nothing you can say——"

"Yes, I need to——"

He shoved at me. He was bigger, taller, stronger, and I stumbled back to hit the wall opposite, and his mood shifted from anger to horror.

"Shit," he cursed, and then immediately the anger

was back. "I'm going inside," he muttered and took a single step from me.

"I'm gay," I said.

He turned to face me, accusing, staring right through me. "And?"

"I'm the last person to judge. Come on, Alex, listen to me, will you?" I was fucking this up so badly, but there was something here with Alex that I was missing. This wasn't just defending Ryker or taking some kind of stance on equality or even reacting to the racial slurs that he experienced. This was a much deeper fear with anger tangled inside.

And abruptly, I knew.

FIVE

Alex

HE GRABBED MY ARM, his fingers biting into my biceps with authority. I paused, hand resting on the handle of The Crimson Cactus, the door cracked, the *thump-thump-thump* of a popular Ariana Grande song pulsed out into the street.

I threw him a dark over-the-shoulder look.

"It's okay," he told me, his words slipping around the lyrics, the shouts of pumped-up patrons, and the cloud of apple-scented vape smoke that was pouring out of the dance club. "Your secret is safe with me."

The inside of my head suddenly became the bridge of the Enterprise on a red alert. Crimson lights flashing, grating siren blasting out of all the com stations, a captain shouting, "Shields up! All hands to battle stations! Load the photon torpedoes and ready to fire on my command!"

"What the fuck are you talking about?" I snarled—the first torpedo fired right across his bow as I slammed the door shut, then spun to face him. He wasn't mad or intimidated by the bigger, stronger, angry Latino stepping into his space. "I don't have any secrets. I'm an open fucking book."

"Of course you are." He slithered around me, yanked the door open, and went inside, leaving me staring at his lean back until he was swallowed up by the crowds. I glanced down the street, then skyward, my sight locking onto the millions of small moths beating themselves to death on the streetlight.

"Fuck him. Fuck him. He knows nothing," I muttered to the insects doing a death dance above my head.

What if he did? What if his gaydar was sounding off?

Gaydar. How stupid. As if. I'd never gotten any kind of vibe off another man. Ever. Not even the ones I knew were into men like Ryker, Tennant Rowe-Madsen, or even this Sebastian dude. Still, if it were a real thing and Sebastian had it, I needed to nip any questions he may have had in the bud. Fuck. I so hated this. Hating it didn't keep me from doing it, though. I wiggled into the skin of a straight Latino man, pasted on the smile the ladies liked, and sauntered into party central. And just like those poor moths outside, the women flocked to me. Some I knew, many I didn't. The combination of booze, loud music, and pro athlete was a lethal draw. By the time I reached the table where Ryker, Colorado, Vlad, and Jens were seated, I'd lost my suit jacket but gained a blonde.

"To the only man I know who can have a lady on his arm *before* he takes a seat." Ryker snorted, lifting his bottle of beer in a salute.

The others joined in, the giggly blonde on my arm blushing and rubbing her hand over my chest. I lifted the cold one Vlad passed to me, drank some, and then led Ms. Booty out to the small dance floor, one hand on her lower back, the other holding my beer. When I turned, my gaze made a fast round of the room. Sebastian was seated at the bar, his gaze on me, his expression inscrutable. Fuck that enigmatic Brit and his stupid secrets.

I leaned down to whisper something into my dance partner's ear, my eyes locked with Sebastian's.

"You're the prettiest woman in here," I told her, sliding an arm around her waist, leading her curvy body closer to mine. Sebastian sipped at his drink, something in a tumbler with a few ice cubes. "You come here all the time?"

"No, first time! Oh my God, you hockey players are so sexy." She fell into me, big breasts tight to my chest, red lips skimming along my jawline, long nails slipping into my hair. "I bet you have a big stick."

I snickered, patted her ass, and then twirled her around so that she was plastered to me, her back to my chest. She squealed in glee when I pulled out my phone and held it over our heads, tilting it to the perfect selfie angle. Her lips morphed into automatic duck lips, which made me want to scream, but I smiled wider, making sure the dimples showed, and I snapped several images. Then, because I was a gentleman, I let her choose the best one.

"This one, Alex, this one! You can really see how great my tits look tonight."

Before my mother's or Father Delgadillo's voice could sound off in my head, I hurried to post the shot to my Instagram page. I added a short explanation:

Ricky Martin isn't the only one! #Latino #player #Raptors

#livinlavidaloca   #hockeyplayersgotallthemoves   #crimsoncactus
#dancedancedance

CamelPhat's newest blared to life. I kept her out on
the dance floor through two songs, leading her back to
the table, then helping her to get her ass into a seat. Not
an easy task, as she was one drink away from spilling
onto the floor. Gaze darting around the packed bar, I
found the seat where Sebastian had been sitting. Some
big dude was sitting there now. As my dance partner
began fawning over Vlad, I slipped away, giving the guys
a nod at my watch, then inching from the table.

"Dude, hold up!" Ryker shouted over a hot number
by Dog Blood.

"Uhm, what am I to do with this?" Vlad asked,
jerking his chin at the blonde now sound asleep in
his lap.

"Get her into a cab," I yelled as blue and green
lights rolled over the sweaty crowd.

I tossed a twenty to the table, clapped our captain on
the shoulder, waved at Jens, and made a beeline for the
door. Ryker fell in beside me, dancing along to the music
until we were outside, and even then he continued
shaking his money maker. Dude had moves, I had to
give him that. The two of us blinked at Colorado exiting
a skinny alleyway, a crude smirk on his rock star pretty
face. A dude and a chick stumbled out into the glow of
the streetlights on our goalie's heels, both tugging their
clothes back into place and blushing madly when they
spied us gawking at them.

"It's got to be the tats," Ryker commented as
Colorado gave us a wink before going back inside to do
whatever it was he did at night. Drink and fuck multiple
people of every and any gender. Great. I was still

carrying my V-card in my wallet, along with a condom my older brother had given me before I'd left for college. Life was so unfair.

"Everyone loves a rock star." I sighed, feeling dirty and sticky like a fly strip in a seedy brothel. Ms. Booty's perfume clung to my skin. It was musky. I needed a shower.

We walked back to the barn, Ryker blathering on about some new third-person shooter game that he thought we should all start playing. His nose was buried in his phone so I could let the Alejandro the Playah Persona drop a bit.

"… called Mecha Metal Corps Elite. Look at the graphics." He waved the cell in front of my face while we waited for the walk signal at the corner.

"Sharp." How had Sebastian known I was gay? Was that even what he meant? Secrets. What secrets?

"We could form a squad and play against other players. Playing games together is a real team-bonding experience. The Railers play *Pokémon Go*, and it really helped them come together as a team."

"We're not the Railers, Ry." Did I look gay? Act gay? Smell gay?

"Well, duh, I know, but we will be someday, and the first step to building that kind of family dynamic is to work on team-building shit. Like this!" Again, the phone was shoved into my face. "There's a phone app game that we can play on the road, and there's a game for the PC or your preferred game system. We could get some of the guys to sign up. You can have twenty people in your battalion. Then you go out in squads of four to blow the shit out of other players."

"You know those violent video games are the cause

of all the mass shootings in this great country of ours, right?"

He gave me a stone-cold glower. "Yeah, no. I think not." We crossed the street, the mirrored sides of the Santa Catalina Arena now in sight. "So, you onboard? We could get Henry signed up too. Then he could play with the team when we're on the road. That will make him feel more connected to everyone." He'd hooked me with Henry. I loved gaming, I really did, but I'd never been big on those MMO type of things, preferring to play by myself to unwind. "Well?"

I looked over at him. Curls hung into his expectant eyes. If he hadn't been taken, and I was living somewhere instead of the back of the closet, I'd have totally asked him out. But he was and I was, and so it was friendship, which, more than likely, was the better option. Romance was for other people, out people, who could experience love and sex openly.

"Sure, yeah."

He pumped the dry air with a fist, then punched me as hard as he could in a friendly you-rock! sort of way. Still hurt. "Awesome! Okay, so when we get home, you download the app, and we'll get you set up. I have my mech suit ready. Check this bitch out! I chose sterling silver for the primary color, then added a touch there on the com panel."

We stopped by my Jeep. Yes, the mech suit was cool. Silver. Big guns. Then I spied the small bi flag over the com panel that housed the communication uplinks for his mechanical war suit. My gaze flew to Ryker tossing his bag into the back of my car.

"You put the bi flag on your mech suit?" I asked,

watching him for any sign of concern or uneasiness. There wasn't any.

"Sure, yeah, why not? It's part of who I am, and it lets the other LGBT players out there know that I'm one of them. When you make yours, you can personalize it as well."

"What are you saying? That I should put a rainbow flag on mine or something?"

He never flinched at my outburst. "Dude, you can put whatever on your suit, and I will not care. Wear the bi flag or the trans flag or the rainbow flag. Go with nonbinary, pan, omni, which I totally think Penn is because he once said he would fuck an alien as long as they didn't have tentacles, because he has a tentacle thing. Wear the ace colors on your helmet. Whatever flag you fly, wear it, and I will be cool with it. And hey, if you're straight, I'm cool with that as well. Just be you, okay, the *real* you."

I glanced up at the reflective sides of our rink. "Yeah, I can't do that," I whispered as he started prattling on again over the new team game idea.

"… tomorrow you hit up Vlad about setting up the battalion, and I'll run it up the flagpole and see if Coach salutes." I threw him a flat look. "See what I did there with the flags and the flagpole."

"*Burro.*"

"I know that one! That means donkey. Hey!"

"Get in. I want to go home and get some sleep."

SLEEP DIDN'T COME EASILY. It teased, and it tempted, dancing just out of reach all night with worrisome questions about Sebastian and his knowledge of my "secret." The longer the night wore on, the edgier I grew. By the time the morning was pinkening the sky, I was wound tighter than a monkey in a *piñata*, to quote my cousin Héctor.

The road trip done we headed home, but even back in Tucson, Ryker was bouncing around the house, all sorts of cranked up about this stupid game idea. I could barely stay awake long enough to eat my eggs and wheat toast. I stopped at the same coffee shop where I'd been last night with Sebastian and slammed back a jumbo Death by Latte, the jolt of all that caffeine might get me through morning skate. I wished we had optional skates, but we sucked far too badly to have the option of ditching any kind of practice. Nerves twanging and hands shaking, I bolted into the dressing room, wired for sound.

Vlad glanced up from tying his skates, his pale blue eyes going round when I flung myself at him like a squirrel on diet pills.

"Hey, so we have this game thing Ryker wants to do. Guns, mech suits, explosions." I made the sound of a bomb going off, then flung my hands in the air to illustrate the big bang. "Team-bonding shit like the Railers do, totally fun. Character creation is max, so you can make your suit with a Russian flag on it!"

"I'm an American now."

"Oh. Okay, well, go with the stars and stripes. Ryker put a bi flag on his. Not that I'm saying you're bi because what do I know?" I snorted, pushed my hair from my eyes, and squinted at him. "You look like that guy in that movie! Yeah, shit, he was this boxer. Rocky fought him. Dude was enormous. Cheekbones you could set a bowl of *queso* on! Blond guy like you, same kind of hair, all short and military, stern. His eyes weren't as pretty as yours. Not that I spend time checking out dude eyes. Man, I am cranked. You ever have a Death by Latte over at the Beanery Depot? Shit will make your eyes sweat and your balls wither."

"Your crash is going to be painful," he said, his deep, deep voice soothing in an odd sort of way. "Also, I don't drink coffee, only herbal tea. As for the game, why are you telling me about it?"

"Tea? No way! My *abuela* drinks tea, but sometimes when she's feeling frisky, she sneaks a little fireball into it!" I slapped his thick arm soundly, then began to snicker. "She's like up to your kneecap, gray-haired, but can kick your ass. I shit you not. Total badass."

"Alejandro, I'm hoping you'll get to the point of this soon. My morning has been… upsetting."

"Duuuuuude, did your girlfriend find out that you put that blonde chick into a cab?"

"No, she simply could not take being with a hockey player."

He sat up. I followed suit. My head swam. "So she left?"

"Yes, gave me her key and packed up this morning. Hockey is a cruel and demanding lover." He sighed, stood, and looked down at me. "She's not the first one to go because of this sport coming first, and she will not be the last." I looked up, up, up at him. What did they feed Russian babies that made them grow so tall? "Men and women come and go. It's the life on the road that kills romance."

"Sorry, Vlad." Tears welled up. I dashed them away. "I uhm… are you cool with us setting up a team for this game? We'd like to have the captain behind us."

"Yes, of course. We need to find things we enjoy and can engage in as a team. This should be run past Coach as well." He ruffled my hair, then thumped off, his skate guards shielding his blades from the floor.

"Yeah, Ryker's talking to him," I called from my seat in front of Vlad's cubicle. He lifted a gloved hand in understanding before he disappeared.

I shot to my feet, paced the room for several minutes, my nerves jangling, my mind whirling with a thousand problems until it settled on one. Sebastian and my secret. What did he mean by that? Ten minutes passed, other players came in and changed out of their street clothes into hockey gear. I barreled out into the corridor when Jens commented on the fact that I had one shoe on, one off, and my shirt had last been seen in the showers. How or why? Not a clue.

"I'm going to go see a man about a secret."

Jens nodded dully, his long dark hair framing his round little face. Cute face. Nice guy.

Where was my phone? Fuck. Whatever. I bolted out of the dressing room, ran into an equipment handler, asked him to forgive me, and spun in a circle as my heart began to pound like a steel drum. I had no clue where to find Sebastian or even if he was here, but I figured I could start upstairs, way above the ice, where the owners were to be found in fancy offices. I really did have to locate him before he started talking to other people about my secret. If he told anyone about it, I'd have to kill him and hide his body in the ice.

I'd seen a magician on TV do that once. Not kill someone, obvs, but hide a person in the ice. Magic ran in my family. My *abuela* said she could charm people into falling in love with just a whispered spell. She was a *bruja* and a good one, according to her, so we kids had always listened well to her in case she got angry and turned us into a horned lizard. Oh, my head was hurting. There were too many thoughts in it. I stumbled to the nearest elevator, stepped inside, and rode it all the way to the top floor of the arena.

Padding along with one sock foot and one shoe foot, shirtless, I began rapping on doors. There were so many of them, all kinds of suites for corporations and rich people with more money than brains. Or was it eggs? *Cerebros o huevos?*

"Alex?"

I jumped and twisted around in the air like a cat chasing a laser. When I landed, Sebastian was there, a foot away, looking whiskery and smelling good. Much better than Ms. Booty last night. He wasn't wearing a suit, just a flowy white shirt and tan slacks. My gaze found a few dark hairs peeking out of the V of his button-down shirt. "Why are you up here without a shoe? Aren't you supposed to be on the ice with all the other blokes?"

"My secret is a secret!" I stated with vigor. "I don't know what you think of my secret, but it's mine, and I don't want anyone else to know my secret."

"I never planned to reveal my assumptions to—"

I reached out to touch his face, the whiskers that were so neatly groomed—designer scruff. Ah, fuck, but it felt wonderful. He wet his lips. My brain met up with my libido in the middle of my chest. I grabbed his chin, yanked his mouth to mine, and felt my heart explode.

SIX

Seb

For a moment, all rational thought fled, and then the danger of what was happening slammed into me. I manhandled Alex into my office and slammed the door behind me, hoping to hell that no one witnessed what had just happened. Alex stumbled backward, gripping me to steady himself, his dark eyes wide, his lips parted, and lust sketched on his expression. He pulled hard, and I overbalanced, even as he met me in the middle, and we tumbled arse-over-tit, landing half on the sofa but mostly on the floor. I shoved him away—this was not the time to kiss a man in my office, particularly when it was Alex, and when there was nothing casual about it. He reached for another kiss, and I held him away while at the same time pushing a desk chair with my foot so it was wedged against the door. I was in the only office on this floor, shoved up in the empty space so I could think, but still, anyone could walk by.

We were at an impasse, me not knowing what the bloody hell was going on, him staring at me as if I was dinner and he was starving. We were both breathing hard, but at least he'd stopped trying to kiss me, and I don't know how long it took, but the desperation and anger in his eyes diminished until abruptly his thought process cleared. As soon as it hit him what he'd done, he scrambled back from me. Weirdly, all I could focus on was that he had one shoe on and no shirt. He reached the wall and drew up his legs, wrapping his arms around his knees and burying his face in them.

Had he been drugged? Was he drunk? What the hell had just happened? What was it that happened that meant he wanted to act on the things he kept inside? Was he trying to prove a point? Did he hope to catch me in a compromising position, scream abuse, and get me fired?

"Alex?" I asked all those questions in just the one single word heavy with meaning, and he stared up at me, his eyes brighter, clearer, and his movements slow.

"Fuck my life," he murmured and then scrubbed at his eyes. "Fuck," he repeated.

I scooted back to lock the door, thankful I'd not raised the blinds in the small window yet. No one needed to witness what was going on with Alex.

"It's okay," I reassured him and waited for him to nod in agreement and then leave me to the rest of my day.

"It's not okay," he mumbled and then cursed in Spanish. The extent of my Spanish was to ask where the bathrooms were, but given the feeling in the tone, I assumed it was a curse of sorts.

"What happened?"

"You." He waved at me and sighed. "With your face and your stubble and everything."

Okay, so he still wasn't making a lot of sense. "I happened?"

"And caffeine . A *lot* of caffeine."

We sat in silence a moment longer, but abruptly, in a flurry of motion, he stood, and I got my first real look at shirtless Alex. His skin was smooth, but he didn't have a six-pack like some of the older players. He was all muscle though, but on the slim side, not bulked up at all. Given that I was still nursing an erection after being jumped and kissed to within an inch of my life, I really shouldn't have been looking.

"Shit, practice." He was wild-eyed again.

I held up a hand and reached for the phone on my desk, putting a call in with Coach, who answered on the first ring with an irritated yes.

"Just to let you know I was talking to Alex in my office and kept him too late. He's on his way down to you now. All my fault if he's late."

"If he's not here in one minute…" Coach huffed and then disconnected the call.

I turned to talk to Alex, but he was scrabbling with the lock, and I watched as he stumbled out of the door. He didn't turn to talk to me, and at the speed he was moving, it was a wonder he didn't fall over his own feet. With a sigh, I watched him leave, then propped the door open. Work was calling, and I couldn't sit around wondering what in God's name had just occurred.

"Can we talk?" Jason asked from the door, and I gestured him in. He sat in the seat that had been propping the door open, and slumped low. Had he heard what just happened? How could he have? Why was he in my office this early on a Tuesday?

"What's up?" I closed my journal and gave him all

my attention. I might've been volunteering my time here, but he was my boss, kind of, and he looked as if the world was bearing down on him.

"The usual shit," he muttered. "Lankinen is appealing his sentence, medical reports…" He stopped then and reached back to shut the door. What the hell people would do if I had a bigger office I don't know. "Henry isn't doing so well. It's his eyesight." He pointed at his face and gave another hearty sigh.

I'd not seen my friend this despondent since he'd broken a leg in the second year at Cambridge and missed trying out for the rowing team. Then I'd nursed him back to health with the promise of sex and drink. Neither with me, of course—Jason was all about the boobs and straight-up whiskey. I was more interested in Nicky the bartender and staying sober so I could enjoy an inevitable blow job after Nicky had finished working. Jason had soon snapped out of the slump, but this wasn't something I could fix easily with drink and sex. So I put my business head on and took the items one at a time, thanking the heavens we weren't discussing, on serious terms, me kissing Alex or Alex kissing me. I doubt Jason would've been cool with me getting up in any player's space if it caused trouble.

"Okay, so Lankinen, on what grounds is he appealing?"

Jason shrugged. "Fuck knows. It's all legal speak, and our lawyer says he has no case and that it will be thrown out, but I had to leave the meeting because he actually suggested we come to a sort of compromise so that Aarni just leaves this alone."

"What kind of compromise?"

"He said himself it was all noise, but I left after

Mark ripped a strip off the lawyer and then stormed out. I followed him, but he was gone, which left Cam sitting there with Mr. Suit. So now I have to find one brother to calm him the hell down and go back and rescue Cam from the boardroom."

"But you came here instead?" I'd known Jason long enough to read his expression. "To talk? Or to hide?"

Jason straightened in the chair and looked indignant for a brief moment before subsiding again. "Maybe a bit of both," he admitted. "It's actually the Henry thing that's messing with my head. The kid is still working through the accident, and it's hit-or-miss whether he will make it back for the next season. I liked Henry, quiet, but he had this funny side…" Jason stopped talking, and I waited a beat to see if he was simply thinking out loud. "How do we deal with this? What are you doing?" he finally asked.

"Ah, so now we get to it, you want to know how I'm going to fix all this?"

"Maybe."

"I'm not, at least not yet. I have preparation to do, but I have a couple of good ideas, one being Alejandro Santos-Garcia, Alex, as our clean-cut poster boy for the Raptors."

I recalled the kiss and wondered if everything I'd come up with was going to lead to the motherlode of bad ideas.

"Alex? But he's… What about Ryker? We bought you in to work with him on—"

"Of course Ryker is part of this, but his personal situation comes with its own, let's say *drawbacks*, with him so closely aligned to"—I looked down at my notes—

"Tennant Rowe. Also there is the fact that he's in a relationship with another man."

"Seriously? We're going there? You're gay for fuck's sake."

That was the second time someone had misunderstood my statement, and I leaned back in my chair, twirling my pen. "Let me tell you a story."

"Jeez, do you have to?"

"In England, we had a footballer Justin Fashanu, who came out as gay—"

"I know this story—"

"—the pressure was intense from the start, from journalists, family, and fans alike. He ended up getting so much hate, and you know how it ended when he took his own life. Do you really think men's professional hockey in the US, a predominantly aggressive and masculine sport, will look kindly on a player who doesn't have the requisite blonde woman on his arm?"

"Well, no, but yes, I mean… What about the Harrisburg Railers? They have so much rainbow on their team it's like they have a pet unicorn at the arena."

"And that is my issue. See, the way it works is the Railers have Tennant Rowe, a phenom who puts up the points. The team is successful, and they already have one Stanley Cup in their trophy cabinet." I was getting proud of my hockey knowledge now. "How many of these championships have the Raptors won? In fifty years?"

"None," Jason said.

"All I am saying is, fans will forgive a lot if the team is winning, but the Raptors? I know they're heading in the right direction, but we need a very different approach, one that plays to the market out there. I want to get Ryker and Alex challenging each other, filming the results, working on Instagram and Twitter. I'd include Henry in this, with his recuperation maybe, if you and the medical staff felt it was appropriate. I want people to see the heart of this team, the friendships that survived even Aarni Lankinen and what he did. I need to see his and hers Halloween costumes with the hockey wives. In fact, I need the hockey wives to step up and create a group to dazzle anyone who follows the team. And definitely, above all things, we need lads being lads. You know—messing about, pranking, challenges, photos of them buff on a beach, playing volleyball. But most of all, scoring goals and winning games."

"Lads being *lads*."

I sighed, Jason had spent four years in England and was one of the only people in the US I knew who didn't need a translation, but I gave it to him anyway. "You know—buddies, messing about, team bonding like that."

He raised an eyebrow. "I know what lads are. I even know what a wardrobe is and a pavement, not to mention I support Manchester United, and drink tea more than coffee now."

I couldn't help laughing. "See? It only took me four years to move you to the dark side."

"Ha, freaking ha." Then he grew serious again. "So, what do we do next?"

"I'll have a report with costings by the end of the week. Three more days and I'll present it to the management team, okay? But first off, you need to hunt down Mark and get him back in the boardroom and rescue Cam."

He huffed, but he left the office, and I realized that

in the space of less than thirty minutes, I'd had two emotional clashes in this small space.

I really need to get out of here.

MY EXPLORATION TOOK me to the kitchens in the basement, one of the places I hadn't visited properly yet. That was where I met Alan and Mo, who ran the space with an iron rod. The team was made up of mainly young kids, apart from them, and I'd eaten some of the food they'd prepared, and it was way better than average for a place like this. Only I thought they were missing a trick, and that was where I guided the conversations when I heard that Alan had trained in France for two years and was a gifted pastry chef and that Mo, his wife, was a genius when it came to decorating cakes. Yet they'd ended up in the dungeons of the arena, turning out healthy food.

"Have you ever considered expanding?" I asked them when I had them both in one room. They were in a lull before the post practice lunch rush, when Alan would prepare specific food for particular skaters.

I wonder what kind of food Alex likes? Is he a dessert person? Cream? I wonder if he likes cream.

"… so yes, we'd like to do that." I caught Alan finishing and realized I'd missed all of it. I tapped my ear and put on my best British accent.

"Apologies, can you repeat?"

Thankfully Alan didn't take issue with the fact that I'd gone off into my own little world. If anything, he seemed to grow more excited by the end of the chat.

A coffee shop for visitors, specialty cakes for events, maybe hosting said events against the backdrop of the arena, with hockey players. I scribbled down the ideas and made a note to look into how other arenas pulled in extra money. I'd assumed there would be vendors selling all kinds of things on game nights, but the information I had was that the major brands weren't interested in buying into the Raptors.

I really wasn't surprised.

We could have a Ryker coffee, sprinkles with his number, an Alex cappuccino with spices, and I knew that this was the small stuff, but at the end of the day, this was a brand we needed to rebuild.

"Where would you do this?" I asked, and Alan was all too happy to show me, leading me up two flights of stairs and along corridors until we reached a pair of double doors.

"Through there is the lobby for tickets, but in here…" He stopped talking and unlocked the padlock holding the door shut and pushed the doors open. The scent of disuse was obvious, and the place was dark until Alan fumbled with the switches by the door and light filled the space. It wasn't vast, but it would easily hold a hundred people, and I noticed that tables and chairs were stacked in the corner, along with another set of doors with STAFF written over it in neon letters. We walked that way and went into a dodgy-looking kitchen, which Alan seemed very proud of. He patted the work surfaces and spun a full three-sixty in slow motion.

"Some investment and we could use this space for what it was meant for: events, parties, business meetings." He grew thoughtful. "It would need some paint," he added, and his bushy gray eyebrows met in the middle as thoughtfulness turned to worry. "Maybe more than just paint."

"Charity events," I announced.

He nodded. "We used to work with several charities, but it all went by the wayside a long time ago. No money for it, apparently."

"Corporate sponsorship, charity, player events, alumni, this could work."

Alan beamed at me, and by the time I was back in my office, I had so many ideas buzzing that I didn't immediately spot Alex sitting on the sofa. He was dressed this time, with a full complement of shoes, and actually wearing a shirt. I came to a halt just inside the door and waited.

"Can I help you?" I asked after the pause grew uncomfortable.

He looked wrecked and not after-practice or postgame exhausted but miserable. After a while, he stood, and with his hands forced in his jacket pockets, he nodded. "I owe you an apology," he murmured. "And I'd be grateful if you didn't mention what happened to anyone else. If what I did was made public, it would destroy my life."

That may have sounded overdramatic, but I was gay and accepted myself for the man I was, quite the opposite of Alex, who was in the closet and had secrets he wanted to take to the grave.

"What happened stays between us," I agreed.

"You swear?"

At that moment, he looked every inch his twenty-two years, vulnerable, scared, and anxious, and I wasn't sure what to say other than to give him the reassurance he needed. I saw a man who was vulnerable to blackmail, and the ammunition he'd given me was terminal if I chose to speak up.

"I swear." I touched my heart because it seemed like the right thing to do.

He saw the gesture, but he didn't seem any less tense. "Thank you." He nodded and sidestepped me to leave.

At the last moment, I put a hand on his arm and held him still. "Alex, if you ever want to talk, you know where I am, and everything we spoke about would be in the strictest confidence."

"I'm sorry," he repeated, "for what I did to you."

He honestly thought he'd caused me harm, and yes, it could be considered workplace harassment if what had happened was written down in black and white. But I had to make him see that in this case he had nothing to be sorry for. He was a mess of confusion and fear, and my instinct was to make things right, so I went straight for honesty.

"I was surprised, Alex, but please believe me that I was kissing you back."

His eyes widened in surprise. Then he shook his arm free. "Okay."

He didn't sound as if he believed me, so I tried one more thing. "We should meet up outside work and talk about the ideas I have for the team." He blanched and stepped backward out of the room. "Purely work," I added.

He mumbled something in Spanish and then left, and not once did he look back.

SEVEN

Alex

_____

SHOULD I TALK TO HIM? Would it help to talk to someone? Who? Should I go to confession?

It had been weeks, several weeks. *Abuela* would've been horrified if she found out that I'd missed mass for six weeks, confession as well. There were no excuses sound enough to explain missing church every Sunday. *"Dios no puede oírte hablar a menos que estés en su casa,"* she always said. I didn't really believe that God couldn't hear you speak unless you were in his house. I felt that if you were sincere in your prayer, God could hear you anywhere. So if I spoke to him regularly, which I did or tried to do, sitting in a hot wooden box with an old priest who reeked of stale wine seemed a waste of time. I just told God my transgressions and eliminated the middleman.

Which brought me back to not having anyone to talk to about my head shit. Could I approach Sebastian? I'd done my best to avoid him for two weeks. Every time I thought about how I'd kissed him, my gut churned. That had been so bad and so out of character for me. It was nasty wrong, taking advantage of a person like that. What if he decided to call me out, go public with a Me Too story about me sexually harassing him at work? Sweet Mary, what the hell had I been thinking? Sure, his lips were soft and his whiskers rough but still… In all my years of dating I had *never* pushed myself on a girl. My soul was now tarnished, the rusty guilt of being gay had a thick patina of new cruddy—

"Garcia! Did you hear one word of what Novi just said?"

My head jerked up so hard my neck cracked. I glanced around to see Coach Anderson glaring at me. Fuck. I swiped at the sweat on my brow, using the towel to help me gather my shit before replying.

"Sorry, no, sir." Her brows dropped into a tight V. "Ma'am! No, ma'am, sir, Coach. Coach. No, I missed it." When I lowered the gold-and-tan towel, everyone on the bench was flaying me with dirty looks. What a jerk I was. Ignoring the associate coach and the captain? "Sorry, cap," I shouted to be heard over the roar of the Railers fans. Vlad gave me a curt nod, but Coach Anderson's glare lingered, as did the one that I was getting from the head coach a few feet away. Fuck. I *had* to get my head out of my ass. That third period sit-and-stew on the bench during our last game should have cleared my thoughts of everything but hockey, but no…

"I said that Lyamin is not feeling well," Vlad repeated for the moron wearing number thirty-four. Man, my hero Auston Matthews would not have been so proud of his fellow Mexican-American, now would he? I bet he'd never acted this stupid or kissed people without permission. "I heard him speaking to Rowe as I skated past his net. He has a bad cold—you can hear it when he speaks."

"So we're going to take advantage of the fact that their goalie is sick." Coach Anderson shoved a whiteboard between Ryker and me, leaned in close, and began scribbling on it in a bright blue marker. Jens leaned around me to see. "Lyamin is a wall, we all know that, but he's not impenetrable. He's always been a little weak on his glove side, but his team plays tight to cover that tiny flaw. Tonight, he's not going to be as quick to recover when his glove drops prematurely. I want all the forwards to stop trying to find a pretty shot and just shoot the fucking puck. From wherever, from every angle, and keep that puck high. If you're in the men's room and see an opening, drop your dick and shoot the puck."

Chuckles broke out along the bench. We'd gotten used to Coach Anderson, after the initial shock of having a woman on the team. She wasn't shy or overly frilly or soft. She called us assholes when needed, praised us when we deserved, and knew her hockey. Also, she had a way of keeping Coach C from becoming too intense. They worked well together. Pity their team was still a sloppy stew of misfits.

I hit the ice with a vengeance born of fear. If I continued to fuck up, Coach would not hesitate to plant my ass in the press box during the next game. The shame of being a healthy scratch, combined with the boulder of other shit clogging up my brain would surely bury me. My family would call asking why, my neighbors would call, the press would call, hell, probably the Pope would call.

I settled in on Ryker's wing, Jens on the other side

back by the boards as we waited for Tennant Rowe to haul his royal self into the faceoff circle. He and Ryker exchanged this quirky sort of smile. Then both dove at the puck, slapping and shoving until Ryker got an elbow into Rowe's chest that knocked him back just enough for his stick to lift. Then it was a simple shuttle of the puck from Ryker to me, and I whirled around and took the shot on the Railers goal.

It careened off the crossbar, Lyamin's big catching mitt missing the slap shot. The puck flew up into the netting, and the whistles blew.

Vlad, being Vlad, made a round of the Railers net as we reconvened for another faceoff. A low, gruff, and short spat of Russian conversation between the two took place, none of which I understood. Stan sneezed loudly, then lifted his mask, which got us another few seconds of waiting while he wiped the inside of his mask clean, using the thin white cotton gloves tenders wear under their blocker and catcher.

"He's not having fun," Vlad told us as he glided our way, stick resting in his arms. "I'll work the crease and him a bit. You three keep shooting."

We three nodded. My gaze went to Lyamin. He'd gotten his mask back on, and those cold gray eyes were watery and red. Yeah, he was a sick puppy. We'd have been idiots not to take advantage of this gift. And so we did. Every time a Raptor got the puck, he shot at the Railers net, and between the flurry of mad shots and Vlad being a first-class pain in the ass, we got three pucks past the Railers goalie. There was a lot of angry Russian being hurled at the pipes down in the Railers end of the ice.

Tennant made a fancy-ass play that snuck one past

Colorado, but that was it, and we skated off with a win, on the Railers home ice. It felt great. Coach C met all of us inside the away locker room with a smile, a pat on the back, and praise. All except me.

"Garcia, is there something going on with you that I need to know about?" Coach asked as I neared, Ryker on my heels.

"No, sir. The only thing going on with me is focusing on hockey."

He said nothing more, just motioned me along.

"*Jesucristo*," I mumbled under my breath, keeping my stupid self to my stupid self after the game. Vowing to get everything not hockey erased from my mind, I made plans to go to my room and watch game film on my tablet until I passed out. No one seemed willing to talk to me, not even Ryker, which said something because Ryker talked a lot and to everyone. The team was headed to the charter bus that would take us to the hotel, a long straggling pack of tired but happy—aside from me—men.

"Hey, hey, Garcia!" Someone shouted as we walked across the empty parking lot, snow crystals swirling in the wind. I couldn't get back to Arizona soon enough. This snow and cold shit sucked. "Ryker, hey, man!"

Ry and I turned to find Adler Lockhart from the Railers jogging after us, thick furry coat hugging his big frame. He caught up with ease, then shook our hands. I'd had enough of him in the game, all over my ass, trying to smash me into the Plexiglas every chance he got, not to mention how much he worried at Ryker like a gnat in the summer. Still, he was a nice guy, and I knew he was friends with Henry, so that was a plus.

"Good game. Next time we'll kick your asses," he

said, then nudged us away from the bus. "I was wondering how Henry was doing. I've been sending flowers every day. Is he getting them? Does he like them? Does he need anything at all? Like a PS4 or a watch so he can keep track of his therapy time? They have great ones in the new Cartier collection. Oh! A horse. Does he need a horse? They say riding horses is great for building leg strength."

"I'm not sure they'd let him keep a horse at the rehab center he's in," Ryker pointed out, lifting his hand in a greeting to his stepfather and father as they had a short visit with Vlad.

"Well, yeah, sure, not in the room obviously, but outside. I could get someone out there to build a stable…" I stared at Adler in confusion. Was he always this generous? "I know he likes old planes. Back when I was in the minors, his brother Dan used to show me all the models and stuff Henry would build. Kid loved tinkering with tiny little parts. Dan and I roomed together for two years. Then I was called up, and he wasn't. We stayed in touch, though. Great family."

"Yeah, Henry's a good guy," I added weakly. "He's doing okay, I guess, you know. It's a pretty bad eye injury."

We all sighed.

"Fucking Aarni. I should have made more of an effort to find a trash truck," Adler snarled. He clapped Ryker, then me on the shoulder and ambled off, slipping his arm around a lean, dark-haired man in a sleek gray winter coat. I'd never seen so much gay in my life. Watching the Railers flow out of the arena, it hit me right in the face how open the team was and how little shit it seemed to cause out here in the real world.

"I'll see you later. I'm grabbing an hour with Dad and Ten. Then I'm heading to the hotel for some sleep."

I waved at Ryker, the cold making my nose run as I studied how two gay men acted in front of other people. Tennant and Jared didn't make a fuss, but they did touch and smile at each other. Could I ever do that? Imagine how nice it would be to hold his hand and walk across a parking lot. Sebastian would look over at me lovingly just like Jared Madsen was doing now when he glanced at Tennant. I think I could do that...

Hey, estúpido, *did you forget who you were and where you come from? Holding hands with a man in public? Yeah, right. As if your family would ever stand having a queer in the house.*

Right. Yes, reality had just shown up. Shoulders up around my cold ears, I climbed into the bus and made my way to the back where the rookies sat. The ride to the hotel was short. I kept to myself, saying little to the other guys and hustling to my room, where I locked the door, changed out of my suit and tie, and stretched out on the bed to watch video after video of the Pittsburgh offense. My eyes began to burn after two hours, yet my mind would *not* shut down. I pulled on a pair of swim trunks I always brought along on road trips, as most hotels had pools, and slid my feet into my sneakers.

Riding down to the lobby at two in the morning in swim trunks felt odd, but as soon as I walked into the pool room, the chlorine smelling warm, misty air surrounded me. The sconces on the walls had been dimmed, leaving the pool the major source of light. I hit a dead stop when I saw some other guy cranking out laps. I thought to turn around and maybe hit the treadmill until Ryker exploded out of the water, levering his upper half out of the pool, long curls plastered to his head.

"Nice backstroke," I said, my voice echoing in the vast room.

He slipped back into the water; his forearms folded over the rounded edge of the in-ground pool.

"Can't sleep?" he asked.

I shook my head, then peeled my Raptors T-shirt off and tossed it beside my shoes. "You?"

"Yeah, sleep is a no-go," he replied on a hearty exhalation, sliding back into the pool to douse his head for a second. "I think I'm going to crack right in half." He ran a hand over his face. "Being away from Jacob is killing me."

"Did your dad have any tips? Like to help get someone you care about out of your head?"

I dipped a foot into the water, my attitude total nonchalance.

"There's really no way not to miss someone you love. Just have to work through it he said. Still, it's easy for him and Ten. They're together all the time. I haven't seen Jacob since Christmas. It just… hurts."

I rubbed the top of his wet head. "Want to swim a few more laps?"

"Totally."

We did forty more. When we finally pulled our wet asses out of the pool, we were both spent. We flopped down onto a pair of yellow loungers, our suits making puddles on the blue tiles. Snow blew against the tall thick windows overlooking a small courtyard buried in white powder. Ryker toweled off his hair, then his face. I opted to just air-dry.

"What's up with you?" His question was a casual

one, and if I'd been a normal human being, I'd have replied more quickly and with something less fractured. I rolled my head to the left. Ryker had his wet towel dangling over his knee, his left leg bent, his hands resting on his belly.

"Things are tense now, that's all."

He moved to lie on his side, and our eyes met. "You know that you can talk to me, right? I mean, you and Henry are my closest friends in Arizona. Maybe if you told me what's eating you, it would help you find some sleep at night."

I let my wet lashes rest on my cheeks until he sighed in defeat. "There's a thing…" I couldn't look at him, and so I squeezed my eyes shut. "I did a thing, to this… person."

"Alex, I cannot imagine you would do anything so bad to warrant the hell you've been putting yourself through the past month or so."

He had no clue. No clue at all. "I kissed this person. Without consent. Just grabbed and kissed."

"And did this person freak out?"

"No, no, they were cool, but my head is all caught up in that kiss and why I did it. It's eating me up inside, even though he said it was fine and he had been kissing me back." The sound of the pool filter humming filled my ears. "I kissed a guy."

"I picked that up." I cracked my eyes and watched random liquid shapes on the ceiling. "Is the fact that you kissed a dude freaking you out, or is it that you acted without consent?"

"Both. No, that's a lie." The underwater lights threw some funky shapes around. "I like kissing men." Eyes glued to the ceiling and a wiggling dolphin-shaped beam of light, I forced those two massive words out from under what weighed me down like an anchor on my chest. "I'm gay."

"Yeah, I know."

That was not the reaction I had expected. I mean… I should have, I guess, since Ryker was deeply in love with a man and had all that rainbow love at home. Still. I had thought he'd be more shocked or something.

"You knew?" My voice was weak with relief. And that anchor resting on my chest? It felt a little lighter. Like, maybe the weight of a few hermit crabs scuttling off the damn thing, lighter.

He chuckled lightly. "I had some major suspicions that you were at least bi because, dude, you are *all* about that Colorado Penn ass."

My reply took a moment. "*Es en buen culo,*" I replied, then giggled at my own stupid comeback. Yeah, it was a fine ass, but holy fuck I said that to another person. To another dude. To my friend. And he didn't throw up or call the priest or even punch me in the face. Tears slipped down my cheeks, and I let them. I didn't hurry to wipe them away, or pretend I was coughing. I let those tears flow, and they began to wash away some of the toxic machismo so many Latino males grow up with.

His hand came to rest on my forearm. "You okay?"

I blinked, coughed, and nodded, unable to look right at him yet. I dragged my fingertips under my eyes. "I've never told anyone that. Ever."

He gave my arm a squeeze. "Thanks for choosing me. I'm really humbled that you consider me worthy of that kind of knowledge. It's safe with me, you know that, right?" I peeked at him and gave him a nod. He caught me. "So, was it Colorado who you kissed?"

My eyes flared. "Dude! No way, man. He's our goalie. The man has groupies. I've got no clue where his dick has been."

"I hear that."

I sat up, threw my feet to the wet tile, and looked right at him. "It was Sebastian Brown."

"I kind of thought he was the one. The way you two look at each other?" He swiveled two fingers between his eyes and mine. "It's crazy hot."

Okay, that really did surprise me. "Yeah?"

"Oh yeah, every time he sees you, he gives you a long, slow eyefuck."

"He's, like, ten years older than me. Is that sick?"

Ryker gave me a *duh* look. "My dad married a guy ten years younger than he is. There's nothing wrong with being attracted to an older man, especially if you're… you know."

"A stupid fumbling virgin?"

"Well, I was going to say kind of inexperienced, but okay…" I slapped my hands over my face. "It's cool. Hey, it's cool." He moved to sit beside me. "It's fine to be a virgin. Jacob was when we got together."

"Don't lie to me, *amigo*," I mumbled into my palms.

"Totally the truth. And for what it's worth, Sebastian seems like a legit guy. Why not see where it goes?" He stood. I uncovered my face. Ryker tossed a towel over my head. "Just be honest with him. Tell him where your head is at and that he's keeping you up at night fantasizing about his hot but pale British bod."

I whipped the towel at his ass and was rewarded with a sharp crack that made him yelp like a scalded dog. He retaliated by trying to get me into a headlock. That got him a slap to the head. We tumbled back into the pool, tried to dunk each other for ten minutes, and then called a truce so we could go to bed.

I had no trouble dropping off that night. Waking up was the rough part, but I slept on the plane back to Tucson after studying the defensive strategies of a team far higher in the table than we could hope to be. As soon as we landed, we were hustled into another charter bus that hauled us to the rink. There the families had gathered to welcome husbands and fathers home. Ryker gave me a long look. I tossed the keys to my Jeep to him. He cocked an eyebrow.

"Go visit Henry, then go home," I said as I tossed my bag into the backseat with his.

"Hey, Alex, if what you're planning goes south, you call me, right? I'm here in ten minutes."

"Thanks. You're a good friend."

I ambled into the arena, rode the elevator up to the big money boxes, and took a short walk, rich carpet swallowing the sounds of my footsteps. At his door, I paused, inhaled, and then glanced around the doorframe. Sebastian was at his desk, earbuds in, tapping away at a laptop. Fuck, he looked good. Whiskery. Older. Kind. Sexy. Would he be gentle with me and my dumb, fluttering heart? There was only one way to find out, so I stepped fully into the doorway. His eyes widened when he spied me. Out came the earbuds.

"Hey," I said, a brilliant opening line if ever I heard one. "Can we do something with some food, maybe, and, like, stuff?"

One side of his mouth lifted subtly. "Or as we Brits call it, a meal."

"Yeah, that. Can we do that? Eat and talk. I'd like to eat with you."

EIGHT

Seb

"WE HAVE a table booked in the name of Brown," I informed the perky waiter with the wandering eyes and the badge that said he was called Nico. I wanted to tell Nico to stop staring at Alex because hey, he was with me. Or at least, he wasn't *with* me in the sense that we knew each other biblically or even that this was a date, but he was my guest at this midsized steak place. The website claimed several awards and plenty of dark corners for couples to have complete privacy. I imagined that was what Alex wanted tonight, anonymity, food, and maybe a whole lot of talking.

"This way," Nico announced and sashayed his way through empty booths to the back of the room and into one of the designated quiet corners.

The restaurant was quiet, but then it was only five p.m., and we had come straight from the rink. Yet another thing to give Alex his space. I gave Alex first choice of seating, and he slid right into the corner, meaning that when I sat down, our knees touched. He seemed to relax when the waiter left after announcing that it was Emma who would be serving us. That was a relief, there was something shifty about Nico and the way he stared at Alex, but unless we drove out into the desert far away from Raptors land, then there was always a chance Alex could be recognized.

Not a big chance. After all, Alex was a new guy, and the new social media campaigns promoting him and the Raptors weren't anything other than ideas in my journal. Still, I wasn't going to reach over and hold hands with him or do anything wildly inappropriate until I knew for sure he wouldn't be spotted. Right now, we were colleagues grabbing dinner, and that was all.

"Hey, guys," Emma announced her arrival by sliding menus in front of us and filling glasses with water. "My name is Emma, and I'll be serving you tonight. The specials board is up there." She pointed at a small chalkboard a small distance away. "Can I get you a drink?"

I checked with Alex first. Did he drink? Or was he one of the team guys who drank protein shakes and nothing else? At least he was over twenty-one, although I knew he'd be asked for ID, and maybe that was enough for him to decide.

"Just water," he murmured.

I frowned at the drinks menu. Beer over here was so different from the stuff back home. There was no sign of a real ale. It was all lite this and micro that, until finally I saw a selection of craft beers and ordered the one at the top of the list. "I'll take a Yuengling Traditional."

"Certainly, and can I just say, I love your accent," Emma announced, and I glanced up to see a very familiar expression. I could probably write a script for what happened next. "It's so cute," she added. Yep, that is where it starts.

"Thank you," I said, same as always, because I really didn't know what else to say, and I'm too polite to be dismissive.

"Where're you from?" she asked as if the answer would mean anything to her. On my first visits to the US, I would talk about the small cottage in the Cotswolds and watch as people looked at me, and then asked me if it was close to London or Oxford. So I skipped that part now.

"London," I lied.

"Oh cool," she said, and I swear she bounced on her feet. "I love *Four Weddings and a Funeral*. Hugh Grant is *sooo* cool. And you know what? I had another guy in here yesterday from London. I think his last name was Jones or something." She stared at me expectantly, but I knew how to handle that as well. I was the same man who had once asked Jason if he knew Royce Parker, who lived in Pittsburgh, so yeah, it wasn't like I hadn't done the same thing. Only I guess, given that the UK was small, maybe it was more likely I would know some random stranger with the last name of Jones.

"We'll just need five to look at the menu."

She stepped back and smiled. "I'll be back."

What I loved about America was the service, the way you didn't have to ask for water, the attention paid to us, and I expected my drink would be here in less than a minute. Everyone was so efficient, and I loved that. It spoke to my own productivity. Without thinking, I reached for Alex's hand, but he caught the movement and moved his hands out of reach.

"I can't," he murmured, and I picked up the menu instead.

"I'm sorry." I had to apologize because he looked so torn.

Alex checked the offered food, but it was a cursory check, and then he shut the menu. "I'm having the surf and turf," he announced.

"I'll have the same."

"Can I just ask something?" Emma said as she pocketed her notepad with the order. She didn't wait for permission, even though she'd kind of asked for it, and instead launched into a story about how her brother loved the Raptors. My chest tightened as Alex squirmed like a bug on a pin. I wasn't even listening to Emma, but after a few terrifying moments, Alex relaxed a little, and I tuned in to her instead of thinking of ways to get out of here with minimal fuss.

"… and so my brother and his husband were there that night. Poor defender got slammed, and I know it wasn't the first time Lankinen has gone too far. We're all glad he's gone. I bet you are too."

I held my breath. The party line was that no one on the team talked about Aarni—deflection was what it was all about, and I wondered how easily Alex would be able to work around this. I shouldn't have worried when he looked up at her with an easy grin.

"I'm just there to play hockey," he said and didn't flinch when she touched him on the shoulder in agreement. Only when she'd gone did the real Alex come back, but it seemed he didn't want to talk about Emma or the Raptors. "You didn't even look properly at your menu," he said instead.

"There's a good reason for that." I leaned forward

and lowered my voice. "I'd rather spend time looking at you." The words spilled out of me, and I watched him as he dipped his head, then appeared to gather himself and stared back at me.

"Oh," he said as if he didn't have the first clue what to say. Then he tipped his chin, smiled, and his whole face lit up. He was so gorgeous, every single part of him from his soft hair to his dark eyes. "I want to look at you too," he said shyly, and there was less the fiery Alex, who tripped over his words, and more of a calm man with measured speech.

God, I itched to reach over and touch his hand, but instead I gripped my water glass so hard that I was concerned it might crack. For a few moments, we smiled at each other with inane grins, and then his bravery fled, and he dipped his head, only looking up when Emma came back with my beer.

"So, uhm, is that right what you said about living in London?" Alex asked, and for him, I would go into detail because it mattered, and he was actually listening to me.

"Not at all. It's just easier. Everyone knows London, but not many have heard of a town in the Cotswolds called Bourton-on-the-water or even the Cotswolds themselves. They would have seen photos, though. It's all chocolate box houses, but it's two hours' drive from London. I have a cliché stone terrace house with views over the hills. My mum and aunt have the house next door."

His eyes widened. "Wait, you live next to your mom?"

"Yep, she keeps an eye on my place when I travel."

"And you live right in the middle of a field or

something? I mean, I've seen films, like *The Holiday*, where it snows, and everything is tiny with thatched roofs and chimneys and absolutely no AC." He shuddered at that last thought, but he did live in Arizona, where AC was a given.

"I live on the edges of the town, which is a tourist trap, but when everyone goes home and it's just me in my tiny garden with a beer, it's home."

He seemed intrigued, "Do you have any pictures?"

I took out my phone and scrolled for the only picture I had of my cottage, one I'd taken to send to Jason a year ago. It had stayed on my phone, even though I'd purged the photos on there at least twice. I was so damn proud of my place, two bedrooms, one bathroom, a kitchen I was refurbishing myself, and a large lounge with a log burner. The windows were quartered, and the woodwork painted a pale green, and the house itself was Grade II listed, dating back to the seventeen hundreds. It was my slice of England, and I'd never been as proud as the moment I picked up the keys. My house paid for outright. All mine, and I wasn't beholden to anyone. Turning the screen, I handed it to him.

He took the phone and examined the image. "It's so pretty," he summarized and zoomed in to have a closer look. "Tell me about your town. Does your family live there? Do you work there? Do you know London at all?"

I could answer most of those questions easily, but the family one I managed to avoid, as our dinners arrived, and we ate as we exchanged small talk about the team. As soon as I could, I asked about his family, and any nerves he had with being seen vanished in an instant. His whole face lit up as he talked about the entire Santos-Garcia family, about how it was Elizabeth's *quinceañera* soon, and how much it meant to her as she turned fifteen. I could've sat and listened to him talk all day as the Spanish names slid out effortlessly, and I knew that if I was ever lucky enough to get him into bed, I would demand he only talked with the soft vowels of his first language.

"So you can see why I can't tell anyone about *me*," he ended after explaining about the church and his family's expectations. All I heard was of a family that loved him dearly and that I would have given my left bollock to be part of as a kid.

"What do you think they would say?"

"I think they'd be sick with grief."

I heard sadness and resignation, but his tone was respectful when it came to what his parents thought. What must it be like to keep a secret like this? To imagine for one minute that the family you treasured might not love you back just because of your sexuality must be a pressure that was tearing him apart, crawling under his skin. No wonder he wasn't relaxing in the restaurant, and I decided there and then that this wasn't the place for us to be right now.

"We should leave," I said and called Emma over to ask for the bill, remembering it was called a check here and pulling out my wallet for the card reader.

"I understand," Alex murmured and sat back in his chair as if he had a weight on his shoulders that was pressing him down. He looked defeated and more than a little lost.

"Understand what?" I said, but he couldn't answer, and we tussled a little over who was paying as Emma was back with the card reader. I beat him to it, only because I already had my wallet out, and he laughed along with Emma at his defeat, although it was a hollow sound. But as soon as Emma left, he went back to appearing dejected and shrunk into his chair. The urge to touch overwhelmed me again. "Alex? What is it you understand?"

"You're used to men who will hold your hand and not sit like a *conejo asustado*." He made rabbit ears and grimaced, so I guess a *koh-neh-hoh -whatever* was a weird-arse scared rabbit. Which he wasn't at all. He was careful and had a secret that scared him. "I understand why you want to leave and that I'm too difficult to handle." He looked frustrated, and his hands were balled into fists on the table.

"I want to go somewhere else," I began, "where I can hold your hand maybe and just talk to you, get to know you."

"We can't go to my place." He looked pained. "Any of the team might be visiting."

"And I'm in a Westman-Reid pool house," I pointed out. Then inspiration hit. "Let's just drive."

"You'll want more." Alex was stubborn, and he didn't move from his chair. "I shouldn't have done this. I don't even know what I'm doing..." He was frozen in place, and he wouldn't meet my gaze, so I did the only thing I could. I slapped a hand on his fist to startle him, then pushed my chair back.

"Come on, let's talk."

I walked out then, hoping he would follow, which he did after a short while, loping out of the restaurant and checking around him as if he expected the paparazzi to be waiting. I'd seriously underestimated how discreet we had to be, and I could've kicked myself for suggesting dinner in a public place. The car wasn't parked far, and

I waited inside, wondering if he would actually join me. As soon as he was in and belted, I drove away from the main street and headed northwest with no particular destination in mind until I spotted signs for Saguaro National Park, which had to have some quiet spaces, right? Hell, it was the desert, wasn't it?

"Ryker knows," Alex blurted as we neared our destination. He'd been quiet up until now, sitting low in his seat and watching the landscape pass. "He says you look at me all the time."

Shit. I do? "I will be more circumspect."

"No, I didn't mean it like that. He says I look back, so it's not just you. I can't believe I'm fucking everything up," he said and then groaned.

I placed my hand on his knee and squeezed it reassuringly. "No one will notice," I lied.

Hockey players had this whole locker room mentality that made no sense to me. It was all men together, and yes, there were players like Madsen who bucked the trend, but the chat was mostly about girls. I'd heard Alex join in, seen the way he held himself when he was in that room, and it was different from the vulnerability he was showing now. He'd grown so good at faking it that no one would think he wasn't straight.

"See what I got?" He held out his hand, and there was a napkin on his palm, still neatly folded, a phone number in dark pen. "Emma says she has a thing for hockey players, and I took the fucking number." He let out a string of Spanish, and the tone was sharp as if the entirety of what he'd added was one long curse after another. "She told me her brother and his husband love hockey, and I had the perfect opening to talk frankly, and I was terrified."

The sign for the Saguaro National Park turnoff was up ahead, and I indicated and took the turn. The road into it was empty and pretty much like the Peak District or the Yorkshire Moors back in England. The Park wasn't grass and swings but a vast open space of wild Arizona desert. There were cacti here and mountains. The heat made everything shimmer, and we followed signs for the first parking lot, pulling up in the final space, with no sign of any other human around. I left the engine on with the AC running, locked the doors, and took off my seat belt before turning to face Alex.

"I shouldn't have suggested a restaurant."

"I shouldn't have freaked out."

"Maybe we should have booked a hotel room—"

"*Puta mierda!* I'm not doing that!" Alex interrupted, unlocked his door, and fumbled with the door handle, clambering out of the car. I copied him, and we met at the front of the rental, the relentless Arizona sun, even in the evening, sucking the air from me and burning my lungs. I hoped to God that we weren't doing this whole emotional scene, standing in the heat.

"I meant, to talk. Alex, nothing else, I swear."

"I don't trust you. I don't want you to do that. I don't want to do that. I don't."

I didn't see the kiss coming, but I had an armful of sexy Alex, and I stumbled back. I separated us and saw his chest heaving. This was out of control and more than I could handle right now. What we had was the start of a delicate negotiation as to what we did, how we did it, and even if we did anything at all.

"Alex, let's get back in the car," I suggested, and after a moment's pause, he nodded, and we were quickly both inside the cold interior. He faced me when he sat down.

"I'm such a fuckup," he muttered. "Like a teenager on a first date, like a *mocoso* on a first day."

I cupped his face and held my hands there until he looked less as if he was going to run, rubbing my thumbs on his cheekbones and holding his gaze.

"No one has to know, Alejandro. No one." I tilted my head and pressed my lips to his, gentling his instinctive reaction of aggression, kissing him lazily, our tongues tangling, tasting the heat of him for the longest time.

Somewhere between the start and end of our first gentle kiss, he went still, and it was only then that I tasted the salt of his tears.

NINE

Alex

___

As FEBRUARY FADED INTO MARCH, and I was dipping a toe into secretly dating a man, I began to see myself as three separate Alejandros.

One was the Alejandro my family expected—cocky, macho, and super-straight. Then there was the Alejandro my team expected—respectful, macho, and super-straight. The third Alejandro was the one I was slowly getting to know as Sebastian and I grew closer.

This third Alejandro was so different from the other two that it was hard to align them all in my head. Alejandro the third was less aggressive, more receptive, and not super-straight. Of course, Alejandro the third came out when Seb and I were alone or, on occasion, when it was just me and Ryker kicking back at home. The gay man inside me was still far too scared to show any signs of not being Mr. Hetero Chick Chaser when I was outside. It was only inside, with my best friend or the man who was willing to let me kiss him, then stop when things got too heated, that I could let the real me out. His patience was through the roof. Seb never got mad at me for backing out or pushing him away. He never ridiculed me for being such a whiny brat begging for more time while rubbing all over him. I was terrified of losing him for not putting out, yet I was terrified of being intimate with him because once that line had been crossed, how would I *ever* shove Alejandro the third back into his dark, airless closet?

Times like now, even though I was home, was a for sure *Alejandro Número Uno*. And he was firmly locked in the cupboard.

"*Buenos dias, Abueladías, Abuela*," I said, smiling at my grandmother as we had our morning computer talk. Her term for it, not mine.

Ryker fell over my back, his arms linked around my neck. "*Buenos dias, Abueladías, Abuela*," he called right into my ear. I grimaced and swatted at him. *Abuela* laughed. "How are you today?"

"*Ustedes dos son tan guapos! Ryker, pregúntame en español.*"

My buddy gave me a blank look.

"She said we're both so handsome." Ryker blushed. "And that she wants you to ask her how she is in Spanish." Ryker blanched. I whispered the correct words to him.

He grinned, climbed over the back of the sofa, and flopped down beside me. "*¿Cómo está?*"

Abuela shook a finger at us, but her wrinkled face was drawn into a smile. "Oh, *mi niñito*, why do you help your friend cheat on his Spanish learning? How will he ever learn good Spanish if you put the words into his ears?"

We both hung our heads in shame. She laughed out loud, then called us scamps.

"I'll do better tomorrow, *Abuela*, I promise. Shower

time!" He slapped my head, then clambered over the back of the couch. "And I'm using the last clean towel!"

"Loser." I chuckled, then focused on the lean little old woman on my laptop screen. "He's a loser."

"He's a good boy. Like you. Two good boys. Alejandro, tell me, who are you bringing to Elizabeth's *quinceañera?*"

Ugh. Ugh. Ugh. Would she die if I said Sebastian? Yes, she would. She would die of shame and embarrassment, as would my parents and siblings. My cousins would beat me senseless, then spit on the *maricón* lying on the ground bleeding.

"I don't know yet." She glared at me over the top of her glasses. "I don't! *Abuela*, there are so many women who want me. How, how can I pick just one and disappoint all the others?" She rolled her eyes, but deep down, she loved the machismo. She could go on for days about how my *Abuelo* had been strong, possessive, jealous, and firm in his knowledge that certain things were not his place as a man, such as cleaning, cooking, and caring for the children.

"Such a cocky rooster," she chided, her usually happy eyes decidedly unhappy. "You must choose a date, Alejandro. Your sister is being stupid about it and refuses to ask any boy we think is suitable."

"Maybe you and *Mamá* could let her choose her own *damas* and *chambelanes?*"

"Pah, the *damas* are all lined up. What girl does not want to wear a beautiful gown and have her hair done like a queen? It's the boys who are balking, and she is not helping for being so stubborn."

I was eternally grateful that I'd been born male. "I think you and *Mamá* should just let her pick. She knows who she likes. If you don't let her decide, she's going to press me to be her *chambelán de honor.*"

Abuela whispered a quick prayer to the Virgin. "What if she picks someone who the family thinks is *un zorillo apestoso?*"

That made me snicker. "Well, if she picks a stinking skunk, then we'll all have to wear masks. You should let her be with the boy she wants to be with, *Abuela.* Everyone should be with the person their heart tells them to be with."

She stared at me hard. "Alejandro, is there someone who *your* heart tells you to be with?"

I blinked at the tiny little gray-haired woman. If only I could tell her…

"No, *Abuela,* there's no special someone that I'd be able to bring home to meet you."

Dark brown eyes burrowed into me. I began to feel itchy. That denial of Sebastian—of me and him and us —hurt badly. "Alejandro, you are my favorite grandson, *si sabes.*"

"*Si, Abuela.*" She told my brother and me that all the time. "I know that."

"You bring home whoever makes your heart sing, *mi niño lindo.*"

My heart flipped, and my gut lurched. "What if it's not the right kind of person?"

"If the person makes you happy, then they are the right person. Blow me a kiss, Alejandro. I am going late for tai chi."

I blew her a kiss. "*Adiós.*"

"*Adiós, papito.*" She tossed me a kiss. Then the screen went blank.

Kind of like my mind. Had I been reading too much

into her words? Yeah, totally. She could no way have meant for me to bring some man home. I stood and shook off the willies that had made my skin prickle.

AFTER A QUICK SHOWER where I had to dry off with a stinky towel, fucking Ryker, my bestie and I stopped to visit Henry. He was down in the dumps, in pain, and surrounded by flowers from Adler Lockhart.

"Dude, he totally said he would buy you a pony," Ryker teased. That made Henry smile for a moment. "I could see you riding through Tucson on the back of a hairy-ass pony."

"Oh! We could each get one, and we'd be the Three Ponyteers!"

We all had a good laugh, and Henry, bless him, even tried to toss out some jibes, but they lacked heart. That was the core of his problems, well, the emotional and mental core. His injuries, of course, were the biggest issue, that eye becoming more and more problematic as time went on, but he'd just given up the fight. He'd lost his passion for life, and I got that. I really did. There were days when I felt life had its boot heel to my throat. Days that I'd been this close to saying fuck it and giving up. Living a lie was corrosive. Then I'd come to Arizona. I'd met Henry and Ryker, Colorado, Vlad, and our new coaching staff. Then Sebastian had arrived, and I was now living a dual life. When I was with him, the agony of my lies was gone. I could snuggle close to a man, touch a man, kiss a man. When we were apart, I was lashed to those damn three rocks and staring into the face of a serpent.

"… this paintball place tomorrow. Part of this public

relations thing the team has cooked up. Lads looking like lads and all that," Ryker was saying, his jab to my side bringing me back to our visit. "This Sebastian guy, he's got some pretty cool ideas that he's trying to get implemented. Shit like following Penn around and snapping pics of him being broody and strumming a guitar."

"The girls will love that," Henry said, easing his leg up onto a pillow. It was a nasty-looking thing, scars everywhere, bright red ones that would take years to fade. They'd not yet unwrapped his eye after the surgery to reattach his retina. There was no guarantee if or when his vision in that eye might return.

"Yeah, they will. We're doing a paintball thing. Then there's some sort of lake setup he wants to do with Alex here." Ryker jerked a thumb at me. "Because he's the *face of the Raptors*," he said, spreading his hands over his head to make an imaginary rainbow. I lobbed a magazine at his fat head.

"Alex is cute." We both stopped chucking that Nat Geo back and forth. Henry's face, what we could see of it, turned a thousand shades of red. "Pretend I didn't say that. The pain meds for this eye are making me gay."

"Is this a new kind of pill that the world has never heard of before?" Ryker asked, giving Henry a pat on the foot. "It's cool, Big H. Alex *is* cute if you hold a picture of me up in front of him."

I flipped Ry off and gave Henry a quick smile. He waved at me, his blush easing a bit as he slowly drifted off to sleep. Ryker and I winked at each other, got to our feet, tossed a sheet over Henry, and snuck out of his room.

"So, Henry has a type, does he?" Ryker asked as we made our way to the front doors. The security guard gave us a look, but he never said a word. Typical. Bet if I'd come in alone, he would have been all over me.

"Just the meds talking," I countered, stumbling over my own feet as Ryker shoved me out into the warm Arizona sun. "Stop it, man. I just wanted him to know I see his shit."

"Leave it be, okay? Coach is already riding you hard. You really want to get into something with some asshole rent-a-cop?" Ryker dropped an arm around my neck. "You can't fix stupid. Come on, let's go grab a bite. You got this beach thing to go be all supermodel for."

"Fuck you," I barked, giving him a playful push. We jostled back and forth until we were both in my Jeep. The wind whipped hard around the windshield. "You okay with all this?"

Ryker snapped his belt, his curls dancing around his face. "With all what? You being the face of the team? Totally, but I just think you should maybe tell Sebastian that you're... wait, no, that's stupid. He knows you're gay. I'm just..." He shrugged. "You know what. It sucks." He slid on a pair of shades. "The whole thing. It sucks. What possible fucking difference does it make who a player takes to his bed? We're still playing the game. Who we sleep with is inconsequential. I just hate that we're still deemed less than because we find the same sex attractive."

"Yeah, well, add on being a Latino when the whole world hates all your *azteca* beauty."

"Aztec?"

"Brown and from Mexican descent," I explained. "That and gay? I'm fucked." I could explain more, about how actually indigenous people were still a majority, even if their culture and legacy was mostly entirely erased, but that was probably for another day, and anyway, Ryker wasn't an asshole who needed shit explaining to him.

Ryker frowned up at the sun. "That is also total bullshit."

We rapped fists, and I cranked over the engine. We had spoken our truth. That was all we could do for now. I left him off at home and headed out to Silverbell Lake. I was supposed to meet up with Seb there to take some snapshots of me chilling at a local park. Feeding the ducks, maybe fishing, typical day off sort of stuff that he wanted to start flooding my and the team's IG feed with. He'd already done some work with Vlad, and his followers had climbed by over a thousand. With my face and the strong Latino community, he was hoping to jack up my numbers and hits, which would then lead to the team picking up more social media presence. The man had ideas, not just SM stuff either, but deeper things for the team that I didn't quite grasp or care about. All this boy wanted was to play hockey and kiss a certain older Brit.

When I pulled into the parking area, Seb and the photographer were there. Both jogged over to me. My belly tightened when Sebastian flashed me a smile.

"No, don't do anything," he said, waving at the tall man with the expensive camera. "I want this," he said, motioning to me sitting in my Jeep, windblown, with a little Katy Perry and Daddy Yankee *Con Calma* remix blaring.

I took his meaning differently. Yeah, I sort of knew he wanted this—this being me—and I wanted him too.

His lips curled. I sat back in the seat, looked at the bright blue sky, and let the photographer do his thing. We spent all day at the lake. I'd been told to sit, stand, pout, smile, hang out with ducks, try my hand at fishing, paddle a kayak, and make sure I interacted with every fan who approached me.

The sky was purple when Steven Maxwell, the photographer, drove off into the sunset. The park was closing in a few hours, and most people had gone home for dinner. Sebastian sat beside me on the ground, our backs to a fat date palm tree, our bare toes resting just at the edge of the water. Wading wasn't allowed, but cooling off your toes? There were no signs against that.

"I'm knackered," he announced. I snickered. "What?"

"Nothing. I like the way you say things."

"Do you, now? And what sort of things is it that you like hearing me say?" His thigh rested next to mine, his fingers between my fingers, our clasped hands tucked between us. "Just so I know for future reference when I'm wooing you."

"Well, wooing is one." I snorted. He bumped my shoulder with his. "Um, let me see. Faffing, bell end, taking the piss, crisps, candy floss, boot, flannel, nappy, and courgette. It's a zucchini!"

"Bloody American." He sighed.

"Hey, Mexican-American, *novio.*"

He stretched his feet out. He had long toes, nicely manicured. His spiffy loafers lay beside my sneakers. "That's a word I've not heard before. What does it mean?"

I hesitated, unsure of why I'd even tossed out that

word so glibly. "Um, it means boyfriend." His silence was unnerving. "Sorry, was that a total whiff?"

"A whiff?"

"You know, like when you go to hit the puck but you miss it completely."

"Oh, um, no, no, I'd say you hit the puck quite well. I'm just trying to shake off the impact of it colliding with my skull."

Shit. Shit. I'd gone in with the B-word too soon. I dropped his hand and stood, the soft dirt cool under my feet. Seb got to his feet as well.

"Forget I said that." I glanced over at him. He was so beautiful with the final colors of the day on his whiskery face. I ached to touch him, to cup his chin, lick into his mouth, hold him close. "I was just... there wasn't a better word to use."

His hand skimmed across my back, settling on my hip. I stiffened and gave the lake a quick glance. There was no one around, at least not close enough to see us. And it was growing dark. And I really needed his touch, so I listed to the side a bit, just enough to press my hip to his.

"It's the perfect word. It means a man who you have a romantic relationship with," he replied, his fingertips slipping under my shirt to rest on my skin. A shiver ran through me. "That's what we're in, isn't it? And before you say it, romance and sex are two vastly different things. You can have sex and not be romantically interested in your sexual partner at all."

"Right, sure, I know that."

He drew me closer, his hand creeping around my side. I had to fight the need to jerk free, act offended, make a stupid joke about not being a queer. It was so deeply embedded in my psyche. The thought that I'd never get past being so terrified to be me choked me down. Seb moved around me, curling in close, wrapping me into his arms. It felt so good, so right, so wonderfully me, being held by this man, that I lowered my head to brush a kiss over his scruffy cheek. Then to his chin. Then my lips roamed over his mouth. The kiss was sweet and soft, and under a tree at the lake. I cinched him tight, kissed him a hundred million times at least, and felt Alejandro the third glowing like one of the early stars twinkling to life over our heads.

TEN

Seb

___

OKAY, so the kiss in the park? That messed with my head more than I cared to think about. First of all, we'd been impossibly stupid out in the open like that, even if it was dark and the park deserted. And we hadn't stopped at one. No, we'd kept going, moving back into the trees, his pliant body pinned between me and the trunk of a huge, sprawling magnolia, and we'd kissed for what seemed to be forever, while picking twigs from our hair. We'd only stopped when I got a cramp from the awkward position, and we'd fallen to the grass, laughing. Because, hell, it's funny shit to get a cramp while kissing, or at least it was that night. He was away now, on day four of a six-day road trip, taking him to Canada, and I'd never seen anyone as excited as him heading out with the team.

So much so that I wanted to run after him like a bloody idiot. I could just imagine me jogging down after the bus, blindly attempting to get onto the damn thing.

"Hey, wake up, you wanker!"

I jumped a mile in my chair and looked up to see a

grinning Jason in the doorway. Four years in England and he'd picked up all the best curse words, which he used loudly with a fake British accent and always ended up cackling like a moron.

"Jesus," I muttered and threw the nearest thing I had to hand, an empty binder I was labeling. It bounced off the wall next to him, and he never even flinched.

"There's a reason you never played sports, you know," he deadpanned and then slid into the guest chair opposite me. "Your aim is for shit."

I couldn't let that go and tossed an entire pot of paperclips at him, several lodging in his hair.

"My aim is fine," I said and narrowed my eyes at him as I expected retaliation.

He shook his head, and the paperclips fell to the floor, all apart from one that attached itself to a curl. I could've told him it was there, but what would have been the fun in that? He didn't retaliate, only crossed his arms over his chest and watched me.

What is he watching me for? There was a lot going on behind his eyes, and I waited for everything to spill out. I was used to this. Jason was the oldest and all calm, Mark the youngest, whom I hardly knew, even though I'd been with the Raptors for nearly two months, and then there was fiery Cameron, who told people exactly what he thought. Not so much now with his careful, considerate gaze.

"It's Garcia we need to talk about," he began, and my chest tightened in shock.

I picked up my soda to hide my reaction, which was heavy on the guilt and worry. "What about Garcia?" I asked as calmly as I could manage. Fuck. Had we messed things up? Were people aware of him and me?

Why the hell had I thought kissing him in the park was a good thing? I knew he was torn between two worlds, and I wasn't a Neanderthal. I knew how to do the right thing.

Except for when you dragged your man into the undergrowth for a quick fumble.

"You need to sex him up," Jason stated, and I nearly spit out a mouthful of my drink. Instead I held it in. Then I swallowed and placed the cup on the desk.

"Excuse me?"

"I saw the prints for the park shoot you did, all playing to the hockey player who likes to fish and run after Frisbees." He cleared his throat. "But in Yvonne's opinion, he had too many clothes on."

"There is so much wrong with that statement," I muttered, relieved that we were not going to be talking about secrets I was keeping. "Not only is your wife way too old for Garcia, but you wouldn't be asking a woman to take her top off to sell hockey tickets, for fuck's sake."

Jason sank lower in his chair, his cheeks red. "I know, I know, but Yvonne basically said that all the other players are doing it, like on water board things behind boats, and you've got to admit hockey players are built fine." He blinked at me. "That's what Yvonne said, anyway, and you're gay. You gotta see that, right?"

"Out," I said with force and pointed at the door. "And don't come back until you've read every antiharassment rule we have in place," I was saying with a jokey tone, but all I could think of was that actually Alex was pretty damn fine and that the idea of him out on the water with all his rippling muscles on show was making my pants tight.

Fucking inappropriate.

"I'm going." Jason held up his hands., "Like I said, it wasn't my idea."

He winked at me, the asshole, and left, pulling the door shut behind him. I concentrated back on the contact sheet of a photo shoot we'd done with the oldest guy on the team, playing with his dogs in the back garden of his huge house. But I couldn't think, because what I'd said was true in so many ways, and not about the objectification. This whole deal was about selling the players not based on skill but on a social profile.

It was that Yvonne was thirty-two, only a few months older than me, so if she was too old for Garcia, then what did that make me? Ten years too old for the hockey player with the gorgeous eyes?

I needed to get out of the office for air, which was how I found myself hiding in the corner of staff parking, sitting in the shade, nursing a new soda, and thinking through my life choices. No one could see me here, and if they did, I would just tell them to go away. Apart from Mark, who found me because, fuck my life, it was his car I was sitting next to.

"Oh. Hey," he began and startled me out of my thoughts so hard I spilled soda down my top.

"Hello," I replied and left it at that.

"I um… you're…" He gestured at his car and then me and then back at the car.

I scrambled to stand and brushed myself down, knowing I'd likely wrecked my suit trousers. "Sorry, mate," I said and then winced. Mate was such a friends-hanging-out word, and not one I would use at work.

"No worries." He went to get in the car and stopped at the last moment. "You want a beer? Some of the staff will be at my place watching the game tonight. Beer? Snacks?"

I immediately thought of the emergency snacks I'd bought from World Market. Maybe this was what I needed to do to get out of my headspace for a while, by watching the Raptors in their game at Toronto, drinking weird-ass American beer, and eating snacks from home. Or I could go back home and watch the game and worry about what I was doing and whether it was fair to keep seeing Alex and also to stop thinking about how sexy Alex was in his uniform.

"Sounds great," I agreed. "Text me the address, and I'll bring snacks."

Mark shook his head. "It's cool. We have loads."

"Not the right ones," I said with a smile, and Mark didn't reply, gunning the engine and heading out.

WATCHING the game at someone else's place on a big-ass plasma TV didn't make it so that Alex wasn't sexy. In fact, he was sexier on the big screen. Every time the camera panned to Ryker, there he was sitting with him, looking all flushed and edible. But at least here, with ten or so others, I could get caught up in the beauty of the fast and dangerous game.

"What is this again?" Mark asked and held up the tiny knobbly stick. He touched his tongue to the end of it and reared back with horror on his face.

"A Twiglet," I explained for the fifth time.

"And it's covered in?" He waved the tiny snack around, and the distaste on his face was hilarious.

"Yeast extract," I deadpanned, "like Marmite."

He raised a single eyebrow. "And Marmite is?"

This was going round in circles. "Mark, I dare you to eat that Twiglet."

He rotated his shoulders and cracked his neck. "If I die…" Then he pushed the snacky goodness into his mouth, crunched twice, swallowed, and sat there with a horrified expression. We stared at each other for a moment, and then he downed half a can of beer, followed by an entire handful of Cheetos. "Dude," he sprayed orange cheesy flakes everywhere, "that is rank."

"I quite like them," Doris said from the other chair. She was one of the team of cleaners, and she and Mark could often be found in the corner cackling over shared jokes. I liked her for her Twiglet-eating prowess.

"Then I name you an honorary Brit," I announced and took a handful of Twiglets for myself.

Mark muttered something that sounded a lot like *tastes like ass*, but he was interrupted when the TV time-out finished and we were back to the action.

No one had expected the Raptors to win tonight. We were up against a strong Toronto team that had thirty points more than we did at this stage. They were heading for the playoffs, that much was certain, unless they fucked up, and who knew what would happen? But heading into the last ten minutes of the last period with the score at four-one to Toronto, it wasn't likely we'd get a win here or even a point for a draw at the end of normal time, which isn't what they call it in the US. In hockey, if the goals were even, then they did this thing where they went out and played for extra minutes or something like that, with the first team to score winning an extra point. Or something. To be honest, I was happy sitting there eating Twiglets, drinking beer, and ogling Alex.

"My man in a suit," Mark stated and pointed at the screen. "Have you ever seen anything so sexy."

Doris threw a Twiglet at Mark, but we were all too glued to the action for it to become a full-on food fight. Anyway, I could see sexier, and his name was Alex.

"Ryker's line is out again," Mark informed us all, even though we were each of us watching the screen. One of the sexiest things I'd ever seen was Alex going over the boards for his shift. Utter focus and fluidity of motion, and all those other things that the announcers spoke about. To them, Alex and Ryker were a dream team. Add Jens, and the line was the one that had gotten the one on the board tonight for the Raptors. They'd earned the nickname on social media of the JAR-line, something I was promoting as a hashtag on Instagram and Twitter.

Ryker was playing as if he had rockets on his skates, the give and go between him, Alex, and Jens enough to have me dizzy, but they were getting closer until one of the Toronto guys slammed into Alex and pushed him right into the Plexiglas.

"What the fuck!" I shouted, but it was okay because next to me, Mark was cursing the actions of the other team. Toronto had the puck, shuttling it between their forwards, and the camera followed them, but all I wanted to see was whether Alex had made it to a standing position. Was he hurt? Where was he?

"Fuck, do you see that?" Mark said and rose to his feet. I followed suit, knowing that if I could just see around the side of the TV, then I could see Alex. He wasn't lying on the ice; he wasn't hurt. Hell, he was front and center, stealing the puck, up on his skates, passing to

Ryker, who had two skaters worrying him, skating backward, and he pressed forward.

"Go, go, go," Mark shouted, urging them on, even though they couldn't hear us. The noise on the TV was deafening, Toronto unhappy, the Raptors fans yelling encouragement.

"Ryker's taking a shot!" Mark shouted, and we went closer to the TV, Twiglets crunching under my feet as I went from despair and worry to elation.

Ryker drew the two defensemen to him, messing with the puck, stopping dead on the ice, and reversing his direction and speed on a dime, and Alex was free. There was space. The defensemen didn't stand a chance, the goalie watching the action to his left.

At the very last moment Ryker slammed the puck to Alex, who didn't even move. He angled his stick, and it was in. The lamp lit, the goal horn sounded, and suddenly we were only two goals down, with at least eight minutes on the clock.

Mark and I hugged and danced in a small circle, as if the Raptors had won the cup when actually it was one goal that might not mean anything if we didn't get two more. Which of course we didn't, but damn it, we shone for those few bright moments, and even Coach looked proud of Ryker's line, touching their shoulders. I could see Alex's grin from here, the sweat on his face when they panned in, the sheer delight in his expression.

My man was on a hockey-high, and damn if I wasn't there with him.

THE NEXT TWO days were excruciatingly hard. Not because the shots from the park were flooding social media, which meant Alex's image was front and center of everything I was doing, but because I missed him. I wanted to hold him and hug him and make the world a safe place for him. He texted me when they landed.

need to talk, landing at one

That was all it said. No kisses, no explanation, nothing, and my heart sank. Maybe him being away this long had given him perspective, and he'd decided he couldn't take *us* any further. I didn't blame him. He was a player on the rise, with a reputation to uphold and a family that expected certain things from him, but I was the older guy who didn't even live in the US. I was going home, and we'd have the entire ocean between us.

I sent him a reply, telling him I'd pick him up from his place, and added an *x*, just so he knew that whatever he had to say to me, that I was coming to him with hope at least. Then I deleted the *x*. Then I added it back. Then I sighed, shut my eyes, and let the short distance between my thumb and send meet in the middle. It had gone with an *x* on the end.

Then, as is my British way, I started to worry and made myself a cup of tea, finishing off the remainder of a packet of Digestives as I sipped the hot drink out by the pool. Jason came out with a beer around eleven, and we exchanged mindless talk about nothing at all, and then it was half an hour until two, and I thought that Alex would probably be home from the airport now.

He was waiting for me outside his place, a duffle over his shoulder, looking way too sexy to be allowed out at this time of night. I pulled up, and he clambered in, belting up and shoving his bag into the back of the rental, awkwardly and in a rush. Then he faced me and spoke as the interior light faded.

"I don't want to go for a drive into the desert," he announced and paused for a moment. He was breaking things off. I could feel it in my bones. "We should get a room," he said in one big rush.

I went from sad acceptance to surprise in an instant. "I'm sorry?"

"A room." He twisted to face forward. "I borrowed stuff from Ryker's bathroom. He doesn't know. I want to know everything is real, and we need a room to talk."

"Talk?"

"Out of the city, the desert, find a place, stop, get a room, talk, and maybe more. Now, go," he said and placed a hand over mine.

It sounded to me as if he was on the edge, as if what we really needed to do was talk at depth, look at the ramifications of what he was suggesting, maybe even take a step back and find a way to calm down.

Still, when I got the room, after driving for an hour, where we talked hockey and in particular the Toronto game, he was the one to lock the door behind us.

ELEVEN

Alex

_____

I HAD NEVER DONE anything like this before.

Sure, I'd fantasized about it, even gone so far as to jerk off a few times thinking about it. Which was another sin, and something that I should confess about, but I wasn't about to tell Father Delgadillo about that or what might happen here tonight in this bed. A crisis of faith was beginning to take hold. I wasn't sure if I was happy about that or sad, but I _was_ happy to be here in this run-down motel, looking at Sebastian eyeballing the tacky wallpaper. I'd heard rumors about this place in hushed whispers from the guys on the team, which was why I'd suggested it. The sleazy aspect of The Gila Monster Motor Court in reality far outweighed the tawdry whispers passed down from one Raptor to another.

"So," I said, tossing my bag to the floor, my resolve to be with Sebastian tonight in a biblical sense starting to weaken a bit when his gaze left the wide bed and flittered to me. He had such pretty eyes.

"Yes, well, this establishment seems to be a bit

dodgy," he said, waving a well-manicured hand at the bed, wall, bathroom, and ceiling. He made a wide circle, one thin eyebrow arching. "Are we sure we want to talk here?"

"Well, yeah, the guys say this place is discreet." I tugged on the knot of my tie, then pulled it out from under my collar.

"Are you sure you didn't misunderstand? Perhaps they said disgusting, and you thought they said discreet." He folded his arms over his chest, popped out a hip, and hit me with a look that made me smile, just a little.

"No, the word was discreet. Like, if you're looking to do something secret with someone you don't want the world to know about…"

"Ah yes, so an adulterer's paradise."

"Hookers too." I shrugged out of my suit jacket and tossed it to a ratty chair in the corner.

"Yes, of course." He sighed in that rather British way of his. "Perhaps we might be better suited to talk in the men's room of that truck stop we passed. It was probably cleaner."

"This isn't so bad." I began to unbutton my dress shirt, working to appear indifferent and utterly cool. Pity my hands were shaking so hard I couldn't work the first button.

"Alex, what is this all about?"

"Sex. It's about sex! *Estúpido botón de mierda!*" I snapped and yanked, sending the button flying across the room. It hit an ugly painting of a lady on the beach waving at a ship, then fell to the worn carpeting. "Great. Ugh, now I have to sew that back on."

Sebastian walked toward me, took my hands from my shirt, and began slowly pushing the next button through the hole, his gaze locked with mine. My breath got shaky. When the button was free, a wicked shiver ran through me.

"I'm not sure that you're as ready as you think you are."

I grabbed the back of his neck, pulled his mouth to mine, and kissed him into the nearest wall. He squeaked a bit when his back hit the doorframe. Or maybe that soft mewl was in reaction to my cock pressing into his pelvic bone. I licked into his mouth, ground my hard-on into him, sucked on his tongue until he began to melt. Then I broke the kiss.

"I'm ready." I rubbed against him, moving a small step to the left to line up our dicks. I nearly came unraveled when my cock rolled over his. I dipped into his mouth for another taste, a longer, wetter one that left us both wobbly and winded. "See how ready I am."

His hands slipped up my back, pulled me closer. "Why are you so ready now? What changed? I'll not bed you until you're sure you're ready, and not just physically. You need to be one hundred percent willing and prepared for this to happen."

"I am, I swear it. Why are you being this way? I know you want me." I thrust against him. He inhaled sharply, his fingers now biting into my shoulder blades. I teetered on the edge of an orgasm.

"Yes, I do, obviously, quite a great deal, but, Alex, our relationship isn't about a quick fuck in a seedy hotel. You're—"

"Say a virgin, and I will freak. I mean it. I'm tired of being the only one in the locker room clinging to something that I'm not sure I even believe in fully anymore! Why should I let the church tell me what to do when they don't even care about me? Why should I follow some stupid moral code of conduct that's outdated? And why should I care what my family thinks about anything I do when as soon as they find out I'm gay, they'll turn away from me? Tell me why I should give a *fuck* about them and their rules!" He blinked, obviously taken aback by the anger that had swept over me. I stepped back a few paces, leaving him jammed against the doorframe, and dropped down onto the edge of the bed. I was honestly shaken at how mad I'd just gotten as well. "I'm sorry." I coughed, dropping my elbows to my knees as I worked on flushing the resentment and confusion from my soul. "I wanted this to be about us, about connecting on a grown-up level. About me becoming a man."

"Having sex with someone does *not* make you a man."

"Well, what does?" I glanced up from the floor to him. He tugged his shirt down and padded over to the bed. When he sat beside me I let him hug me into his side.

"So many things." His voice was soft and calm; his fingers rested on my shoulder. "How you treat others obviously. Respecting your elders, being kind to animals and those weaker than you, being compassionate. Having integrity, confidence, a sense of humor, loyalty, empathy. Being direct, being honest, being a gentleman. I would wager that if you asked a man this same question fifty years ago the reply would have been much different."

"I'm not confident at all," I mumbled, feeling as if someone had thrown me into a blender, yet again.

"I disagree. I've seen you on the ice and out in public. You have great confidence in your skills."

"There's more to life than hockey. How can I be this much of a mess?" He slid his hand to the back of my neck, his grip tightening, then working the stiff tendons.

"You're not a mess at all, and dare I say that you possess a goodly number of those masculine traits. What you're experiencing is growing pains. We all go through this, but it's sometimes much harder for a gay man to come to grips with what he is and where he needs to go in life. Being raised in a devout family is making your journey that much harder."

"I used to find a lot of strength in the church, but now…"

He leaned over just enough that his head rested against mine. His fingers kept kneading the rock-hard muscles of my neck and shoulders.

"Perhaps you could look into attending a different church. Something more open and welcoming than your current church seems to be to our community," he offered. I made a sound of utter disbelief. Leave the church? *Dios nos salve.* My mother and grandmother would die of shock and broken hearts. "It was just a suggestion. I know your faith is important to you."

"Sort of yeah. It would be stronger if I felt welcome," I confessed, the first confession that I'd been to in months.

And as alarming as that was, it wasn't upsetting me as it should. Maybe I *could* find a new place of worship. Somewhere that would accept me as me. Alejandro Ricardo Santos-Garcia. A gay hockey player with a marvelous British boyfriend. I moved my head just enough to be able to press my lips to his cheek. That soft scruff that he worked so expertly rubbed against my lips. God, I loved that sensation so much. His eyes drifted shut, the fingertips working my neck slowed, then stopped. He rolled his head, his mouth seeking mine. The kissing grew from a gentle, yearning thing into roaring passion in a matter of seconds. The fire was a hot one, one I couldn't contain and really didn't want to. Sebastian took the lead this time, easing me back to the bed, his concern about cooties seemingly forgotten as he nibbled down along my jaw to my neck while his nimble fingers worked on those tiny, pesky buttons.

"Ahh, sweet," I gasped when his hand parted my dress shirt and fell to my bare chest. "Give me more."

He did. With tender touches and sweeping caresses, we discovered each other's bodies, bit by bit, removing one article of clothing, then tasting and touching that exposed patch of skin. We moved across the bed, rolling one over the other, legs and arms tangled when we were down to our briefs. I wanted so much. I wanted him, his body, his smiles, his hot skin pressed to mine. I wanted it all, but I had no clue how to ask for it. Sebastian knew, though. Somehow, he knew how to love me and encourage me to request what it was I needed the most.

"There, yes, higher, slower, kiss me now. Let me taste your shoulder." Simple soft pleas that led us higher and higher, our breaths shaky, our cocks weeping.

"Love the taste of you," he purred, licking his way down my stomach, his hands braced on either side of my waist.

I arched up, eager, like a young stallion turned out among the mares with no clue how to proceed but with a frenzied need to do something, even if it was wrong. But it wasn't wrong; Sebastian wouldn't let it be wrong.

He eased himself between my legs, eyes burning hot when they touched mine, and then ran his lips along the hard ridge of my dick. Even through the thin cotton the sensation was incredible.

"Hurry, shit…" I could feel the tingle in my balls.

"Think about hockey," he murmured, nudging at my dick with his nose, pushing it up to lie on my belly. I trembled and cussed in Spanish when he freed just the tip of my cock, the slick head peeking out of the elastic band of my blue boxer briefs. "Think about anything but me doing this."

Arms resting on me, he took the head of my cock into his mouth. I bucked just like that callow young stud horse, my hips jerking up, my hands wadding the ugly green bedcover. God, he was good, so good, so *incredibly* good. He sucked, using the tip of his tongue to press into the slit, then wiggling his chin to expose more and more of my cock. Each inch that slid free, he swallowed until he had me all the way down his throat. I came far too fast, the white explosion of pleasure starting at the base of my spine was on me before I could even shout a warning. Sebastian moaned as I filled his mouth, swallowing greedily, his hands coming to rest on my lower belly, applying soft pressure as I writhed and shuddered under him.

"Hell… ah hell," I panted, my limbs like jelly, my skull stuffed with batting. Sebastian tucked my spent dick back into my shorts, climbed up over me, and laid his long, lean body atop mine. "That was… you're wonderful."

"Have you ever tasted yourself on another man's tongue?"

"No, never…" A wave of wantonness washed over

me. "I want to." I slid my hands into his hair, then led his mouth to mine. He lapped at my lower lip, then slipped his tongue into my mouth, rubbing my taste over my taste buds. I loved the taste of him, of us, of me on his tongue. He rocked his hips into my belly, his erection a hard reminder that he'd not found his release. I released one hand from his hair and eased it between us, slipping my fingers into his briefs. He hissed when I took his cock in my hand. I stroked the length of him, loving the soft steely weight of his dick sliding over my palm.

"Oh, that is lovely," he whispered into my mouth while I pumped him. "Tighter, mm, yes, now harder… harder… ah shit, yes. Just like that."

When he came, his face was buried in my neck. My eyes were closed. His cock pulsed in my hand, coating my fingers with hot spunk. He fucked madly for a moment, using his cum as lubricant. His dick leaked more and more cum with each frantic thrust. I groaned along with him. His weight settled on me for a few moments as we both drifted back down. Then he lifted his head and slanted his mouth over mine. I explored his mouth, melting back into the covers, my hand still between us, his cum cooling between my fingers.

"Did you enjoy that?" he asked softly, his lips pink and slick from kissing.

"*Dios, si*. God, yes, so much. So much…"

"Me too, so much." He gave me another kiss, then wiggled off me, rolling to his feet. I sat up, my hand a gummy mess, and stood. "Let's grab a quick shower if we dare."

We snuck up into the bathroom as if there was a serial killer or an eight-foot cockroach hiding in the shower. There wasn't. And amazingly, the bathroom was pretty clean. Clean enough for me anyway. Sebastian tutted and tsk-tsk-tsk'd at the towels and the toilet that made bubbly sounds. I was too woozy and glowing to make unhappy mom sounds. The shower was barely big enough for me, let alone the two of us, but once we wiggled in and pulled the curtain around us, the close quarters was just about perfect.

"We should have chosen a more tasteful suite for our first rendezvous," he said as he lathered cheap motel shampoo into my hair. I grunted in reply, too far gone in contented lover mode to even make words happen. I was so in love. Everything about him, about us, about this room and this shower and this shampoo that smelled like the lemon stuff *Abuela* mopped her floors with… it was all just perfect. His fingers massaging my scalp, the feel of his nude body tight to mine. "Something like the Tucson Century Towers. Five stars, massive rooms with superb amenities. That should have been where we made love."

"It doesn't matter to me where it was, just that it was." I turned my face into the water, smiling at the tickle of bubbles washing down over my face, chest, and back. Sebastian kissed me right under the spray. I blinked and opened my eyes to look at him.

"Yes, you're right. All that matters is that it was you and it was amazing for you." He cupped my face, using his thumb to flick off a bit of lather. "You are incredibly special. To me, that is, and I would be proud to be known as your boyfriend if and when the time comes. You're such a passionate, loving, devoted man."

I threw my arms around him, kissing him hard, wiggling my leg between his. His hands found my ass, mine found his shoulders, and before I knew it, we were rutting against each other, once flaccid dicks now iron hard again. He jammed me back into the corner of the shower, took both of us in his hand, and worked us into a hot, wet frenzy. I couldn't take my eyes off the sight of our dicks pressed together, slipping and sliding and bumping. With a growl, I placed my hand around his. We both came again, our mouths fused, water washing the semen down the drain, my hand on his buttock, his planted to the shower stall by my head.

"Well, *that* was unexpected." He chuckled, then dropped a kiss to my chin. "We had best stop faffing about in here. The hot water is growing tepid."

I grinned like a goof. "I really like the way you talk."

"I like the way you talk as well. Now be a good lad and soap my back."

We rushed through the shower because, as he had noted, the water was growing colder. We dressed out in the bedroom after locating our clothes, which had been flung all over the room. He opted to go commando since he'd come all over his underwear.

"I'll just toss these into the bin when I get home. I refuse to rinse cold cum off of underwear. Life is too short." He wadded his briefs into a tight ball, then crammed them into the front pocket of his trousers. They hung out a bit, but who cared? The prostitutes in all the other hourly rated rooms wouldn't look down their noses at us, I was pretty sure. That made me giggle internally. Then sigh, which got a curious glance from Sebastian, who was seated on the bed, sliding his feet into his Italian leather loafers.

"I was just thinking how the hookers on either side of this room wouldn't give two shits about your underwear hanging out of your pocket or even that we're two guys who just got each other off, twice." I held up two fingers, then went back to buckling my belt. "But if my mother saw us coming out of here looking like we do, there would be epic end-of-the-world level judgery."

"I'm not sure 'judgery' is a word, but I'm going to leave it because it fits so well," he tossed out as he stood. "Have you ever spoken with your family about how they feel about gays?"

"Pfft, no, I see how my cousins are. You don't know the Latino culture well yet. Trust me. When you get to experience it firsthand, you'll be like 'Ah okay, now I see what Alejandro is talking about!'"

"I wasn't referring to your cousins. All young males are idiots, present company excluded, of course, so you can lower that brow. What I meant was have you ever talked about gays with your parents or your grandmother. Maybe they'd surprise you."

"Yeah, no, I doubt it."

"Well, perhaps you should broach the subject someday, just to test the waters."

I shrugged, slid my arms into my jacket, and picked up my bag. It was untouched, the stuff I'd stolen from Ryker not used, which was disappointing but not really. What we'd done, the talk followed by the loving, had been perfect. Someday we'd work up to other stuff, stuff that needed stuff, but for now, I was happy. So damn happy. Sebastian opened the door and stepped out to the sidewalk. I rushed him, grabbing him around the waist and plastering a steamy kiss to his sexy lips.

"What the hell?" he asked, his question thick with laughter, as he caught me and pinned me to the dirty brick wall between our room and the room next to ours.

"I'm just happy," I confided. His lips found mine. I clung to him like *Mamá's* pink clematis.

A door to our left opened. I stopped kissing on Seb long enough to glance to the side. All my joy vanished.

"Small world, huh, Garcia?" Coach Carmichael asked, his arm draped casually over Mark Westman-Reid's shoulder.

TWELVE

Seb

FOR SOME REASON, I moved fast to put myself between Coach and Alex. As if that was going to make any difference to the fact that the person responsible for Alex's position on the team was standing there with an inquisitive gaze and whisker burn on his neck. Mark's mouth fell open. Then he shut it deliberately and began to shuffle back, tugging Coach with him.

"Let's go, Rowen," he murmured, but Coach Carmichael was not to be moved.

"Alex?" Rowen asked, all kinds of gentle and encouraging, but Alex stayed behind me, and I heard a whimpered Spanish curse. Coach sighed. "Thirty-four, front and center," he said, this time his tone was firmer.

Alex moved, and this time it was him standing between the coach and me. "Coach," he murmured miserably.

I couldn't for one minute think of the panic in his head. He had to be imagining the worst here. Everyone stood there saying nothing for way too long.

"What are *you* two doing here?" I blurted, even

though it was obvious, because I hated silences with a passion, and they weren't saying a damn thing to each other.

"Anniversary," Mark mumbled and couldn't quite meet my eyes. Given the two men were in a committed relationship, I would have thought an anniversary could have involved something a lot more exciting than a room in this dump.

"This is a personal and private matter," I said, loud enough to catch Rowen's attention. "Let's go, Alex." If I thought that was going to work, I didn't know anything at all.

Alex tensed, Rowen shook his head, and Mark made a face that said I'd just spoken out of turn. Who the hell knew how this player/coach relationship worked, but me suggesting we leave wasn't going down well.

Rowen moved away from Mark and came close to Alex, who to give him his due, didn't move a muscle. In fact he tilted his chin.

"Alex?" I asked under my breath, "Do you want to go?"

"It's okay, Seb," he said, and I mentally took a step back. This was a vital moment for Alex, and maybe he didn't need me getting in the way.

Rowen reached out for Alex, cupped him behind his head, and I tensed, waiting for them to get into it, but all Rowen did was touch his forehead to Alex's and sigh. "It's okay," he said and then backed away.

"It's not," Alex blurted. "I can't do this. I can't be this." He threw me a frantic look.

Fuck. What did I do? What could I say that would make this any better? We were all shocked, Mark quiet, Rowen thoughtful, Alex stiff as a board, and me, flapping inside like a demented bird but outwardly calm.

"Let's get coffee," Mark finally said. "Follow us."

They reached their car, a sleek Maserati parked outside this shit motel, hidden behind the large bushes where we would never have seen it. I couldn't believe it hadn't been stolen. Hell, it was a fucking Maserati among ten other cars, most of which were rentals or old models barely hanging together. We moved as well, but any hint of closeness or connection was vanishing. All I felt was Alex's shame, and it made me ache. He belted up, and I pulled out after the Maserati, wanting to say something clever and important, one sentence that would make the tension leave my boyfriend as if this morning's unfortunate meet-up had never happened.

"You want me to follow them?" I asked after a while.

"Sure," Alex murmured.

"We don't have to, you know. You're not at the rink, not in uniform, Rowen isn't your coach on your downtime."

He shot me an incredulous look as if I'd just suggested something heinous. "You don't understand shit," he snapped. So that was why we were silent for the rest of the journey as I contemplated the unfortunate ending of things. I pulled into the driveway of a modest detached house surrounded by grass and flowers. I didn't know whose house this was, but it seemed we weren't going to get our coffee in Starbucks.

I wanted to make him see I was on his side and made the unfortunate choice to carry on with the last thing he'd said. "Maybe I do understand some of what you're feeling—"

"What? I bet *you* had a perfect fucking family who

probably accepted you being gay like you'd just casually told them to pass the fucking potatoes. I bet you didn't have a mom who worked her fingers to the bone for her family and who prays every night for your eternal fucking soul. Or a dad who works every hour God sends to feed his kids, and wants you to be half of the next hockey power couple with the perfect fucking blonde woman on my arm. I bet no one judged you as stupid if you got a B on a fucking report on the implications of Revelations in the Goddamn Bible! Not to mention, you probably didn't have siblings who have you pushed into a fucking box labeled superstar heterosexual hockey player. Oh, and I *know* you can't have a cousin who hired a prostitute for your fourteenth birthday to show you the fucking ropes! They all want so much for me, and it's killing me, and I'm nothing like you. So tell me, how you can understand any of the stress I'm going through?"

"You're right. My mum understood when I told her I was gay," I said and switched off the engine. He didn't face me. "But she told me right there and then that it didn't matter what I was as long as I made something of myself. The pressure to be perfect, even in a house filled with love, can be stifling. Also, you know what. I never knew my dad. He was posted back to the US when my mom was pregnant, said he would marry her and bring her over. What actually happened was that he abandoned her with her unfortunate pregnancy. The fucker. Actually, my mum lived on a sofa at my aunt Olivia's house, but when I was born, we actually got our own council flat, sandwiched between members of rival drug gangs."

He turned to look at me then. "Seb——"

"You think I had it easy? I stole the uniform for my first school from Tesco. I was five. I don't have siblings or cousins that I know of. Just me, Mum, and Aunt Olivia. No one prays for my soul, no one got me a prostitute, but I worked *fucking* hard to get where I am now, worked my ass off for all the A grades to get a scholarship to university. So yeah, I understand what it's like to have pressure, and no, I didn't have it easy, so don't let the suits I wear or the perfect English vowels I use fool you." My voice slipped a little, and as I spoke, I saw Alex's eyes widen.

"Oh," he whispered. "When you say your dad went back to the States—"

"USAF. He's dead now, never met him, didn't want to after what he did. So don't think that my life was all roses." He winced. *Fuck, I'm being selfish. What the hell am I doing?* "I apologize for that outburst."

Alex shook his head. "You don't need to. I'm sorry as well. I know it's not all about me all the time."

I gripped his hand. "This *is* all about you, Alex, and I'm here for you, okay? I understand what *you* are feeling right now. I know you're scared, but what is the worst that can happen here? Coach won't jeopardize the mythical JAR line, and why would Mark, one of the owners of the team, want to rock the boat?"

Alex fisted his hands in his lap and then cursed loudly. I think he would have said more, only Rowen knocked on the window with force.

"Thirty-four, out," he ordered.

Alex scrambled to comply. I followed at a more sedate pace, anything to give me time to settle my thoughts. Alex needed me on his side, and I'd already considered a couple of lawyers I'd worked with in the past whom I'd call for advice.

All four of us ended up in the large kitchen at the back of the house, Mark making coffee, Rowen sitting at a table, and Alex standing in the doorway as if he was heading for his execution.

"Do I need my rep?" Alex asked, and it hit me then just how messed up this was.

"You haven't done anything wrong," I interjected before Rowen began whatever lecture he was percolating in his head.

"We should all sit," Mark interjected and handed me a mug. "I made you a tea."

I glanced down at the dishwater-colored liquid in a mug. "That's an insult to tea," I said, attempting to lighten the tone. When I glanced at the others, they stared back at me, and I drew myself tall. "Never, *ever*, make tea for a Brit," I added with a smile, then tipped it away and poured myself a coffee instead before taking my seat at the table. They'd waited for me, but I hoped my humor insertion, plus the whole coffee-pouring thing, had lightened the mood a little. Alex was no longer mutinously defensive but scared, and Rowen was less thundery.

Rowen cleared his throat. "Garcia, who you see on your own time is up to you. I'm with Mark, and also young Ryker is visible in his relationship. This team is supportive, and anyone who gives you shit will be shown the door. So, my first real question is actually for Sebastian and how he is managing this."

I blinked at him. Managing what? Sex?

Mark interjected again. He was good at that. "What

Rowen is saying, is that Alex is pivotal to your campaign."

Oh. That.

"Actually, he's only one of many angles we are working," I began.

"I'm not coming out," Alex interrupted and stood so fast from the table his chair scooted back and hit the wall, and coffee spilled over the edge of his full mug. "No one can make me do that or manage it for me." He stared at me in horror, as if I'd agreed somehow that we did a poster campaign with unicorns, rainbows, and Alex in the center.

"I know—"

"What happens—?"

Rowen and I spoke at the same time, and I gestured for him to go first.

"What happens at The Gila Monster Motor Court stays at The Gila Monster Motor Court." Rowen was calm. "Sit down, Garcia." Alex did as he was told and scooted the chair closer to the table. "Who you sleep with is your choice and no one's business but your own, but a word of advice here. You were in a public place. You're known around here to some, and it only takes one person to take a photo, and the message you get out to fans becomes something twisted and toxic. Add in the fact that your poster is on a billboard not more than a quarter mile from the motel, and you have a situation here. Understand?"

He stopped then and sipped his coffee.

"Yes, Coach," Alex mumbled, but I thought it was more a reflex than anything else.

"Also, I want to talk hockey. Alex, look at me." He

glanced up as Rowen continued. "Do you want Mark and Seb to leave?"

Alex was pale, glancing at me and shaking his head. I could see the pain in his expression. He thought the one thing he had right now was going to be taken away from him, and I hoped to hell he didn't send me packing right along with hockey.

"Coach?" he said as a prompt when Rowen went quiet. "Please don't scratch me. I won't let this change my play. I'm giving everything right now."

Rowen pushed his mug to one side and steepled his fingers, staring at Alex.

"Thing is, Alex, you are, and you aren't. You make some amazing plays, but you're easily distracted, and in the same game you score a goal, you'll make a turnover that the other team uses to their advantage. You've got skills off the chart, your speed, your accuracy, the way you so effortlessly work on the line with Ryker and Jens. When you make any kind of magic move, you get cocky, and your focus is gone. Want to tell me why?"

"I didn't think I…" He stopped and scrubbed at his eyes. "I don't know."

"Okay, then answer me this. Who do you play for?"

"The team, you, coach."

Rowen nodded. "But do you play for yourself? Do you love the game? Is it what you eat and breathe?"

I waited for Alex's answer with fear. Of course he loved the game, but right now, what he and I had going on was a distraction, not to mention all the stress he felt for hiding his secret.

"No," Alex admitted after a pause. "I mean, I love the game. Of course I do. It's everything to me…" He stopped, then visibly deflated. "No, it's not everything.

There's too much inside me, and when I score, all I can think…"

He was a strong, determined hockey player, but right now, he seemed vulnerable. Was I doing that to him? Should I just back away and leave him be? I didn't want to. I was falling hard for him, and if I ignored the fact of visas and hockey, I could even imagine a future that was him and me. A few years at least, just until he was ready to go out and find his soulmate.

Of course, it would kill me when we were done and he moved on, but he didn't have to know that. He had a whole life to live, and I was his experiment and had a time limit because I'd be going home. I wasn't going to confuse the situation, so I stayed quiet.

"What do you think?" Rowen pushed.

"That I make people proud of me, that I show everyone that the Latino from San Luis can play in the NHL and make a difference. Fans, the team, even my family, who doubted my obsession with ice in a goddamn desert state."

"Are you proud of yourself?" Rowen asked gently. "That is all you have to ask. Yes, you play for the team, the fans, me, your family, but you have to be proud of yourself as well." Silence. "My door is open at any time if you need to talk because I know for sure that a player is only as good as the determination and pride they feel in themselves."

Alex stood again. "Can I go now, Coach?"

Rowen stood and extended a hand, which Alex shook. Then Mark came around and hugged him, and we all carefully and politely moved apart.

Alex was quiet in the car as we drove back to his place, and I didn't push him, just rested a hand on his knee in silent support. When we arrived, he didn't invite me in, and why would he? Instead, he squeezed my hand and nodded. "Thank you for everything," he said and left.

THREE DAYS I waited for *him* to text me, all the while sending him little messages about my day. Nothing too complicated, details of his promos, a funny story about Colorado and his inability to sit still in interviews, and a link to some hockey memes. In those three days, he attended two practices, and today was the next game, against LA, a local matchup, which had tensions rising in the rink. It was a home game, which meant that a large number of LA fans would be descending on our arena, and it was this game we were using as the focus for episode one of our new behind-the-scenes documentary *Raptors-Radio*, which was a cool name despite the fact that it wasn't on the radio. It had a retro feel. There would be three episodes taking us up to season's end.

Yesterday, after a heated practice, Ryker, Jens, and Alex had done a skills competition with footballs and hockey sticks, on ice. I was there watching the three of them horse around, and I wouldn't have known that the event at The Gila Monster Motor Court had even happened. He was smiling, grinning, messing around as if he didn't have a care in the world, and the footage we got was so good. Enough for the episode, plus some GIFs and stills we could use on social media. At least no one saw me staring at the stills of Alex in my office, at least no one except Jason, who loudly called me a wanker, scared the shit out of me again, and then pointed at Alex on my screen.

"Nice photos," was all he said, but I got the feeling I overreacted with my blustering and shutting the screen. If the look he gave me was anything to go by, he knew I'd been staring. It had been him who'd invited me up to the box tonight, to watch the game in luxury, given as how he was out of town with his wife's family and the box needed bodies, which I acknowledged was good for marketing. So here I was, nursing a beer and watching every part of the game from up high.

Hockey games weren't much like football games back in England. There was no real segregation of fans. Everyone was good-natured, for the most part. There wasn't violence in the seats that I could see, but there was a lot of cheering every single time the JAR line took the ice. I was smug. We were two goals up, both from the JAR line, and even though Alex hadn't gotten the goals, he was certainly getting assists. He was on fire tonight, focused, accurate, and scrapping for every loose puck that came his way. When the third goal went in, this time a give-and-go from Alex to Ryker and back to Alex, I was up on my feet with the Raptors fans, shouting in jubilation.

That's my Alex, out there, being all cool and sexy.

I hung around the arena after the game. We'd taken LA three goals to one, and I wanted to soak up the sheer excitement buzzing around the team. I spent time watching fans and talking to the guys in the Raptors concession shop, noting that it was Ryker jerseys flying out of the shop if fifty-two in one night is considered flying. Who knew, but it made me smile to myself when they told me they'd sold twenty-one Garcia shirts with the number thirty-four on them. There was even evidence on the concourse of grudging respect from the LA fans, although I did hear a couple of curses and the odd mention of wanting Ryker traded to their team immediately. I couldn't see a world where the Raptors let go of Ryker or Alex, but hockey was a weird game.

Then I hung around the parking lot, waiting for the players, exchanging high fives as they came out in twos and threes, and finally I saw Ryker and Alex. They stopped and signed caps and jerseys, joking with the wide-eyed kids who'd been allowed to stay up late for this Saturday game. When they came closer and Alex saw me standing by my rental, he stopped walking and said something to Ryker, which resulted in a fist bump. It was only Alex who came over to me, Ryker getting in his car and heading out.

"Do you need a ride?" I asked.

Shit, that was some loaded question.

Alex nodded and got into the car, belted himself in. "Can we drive out somewhere and talk?"

Dread pooled inside me, but I stayed positive. "Jason's away, with Yvonne and the kids. We could go to the pool house?"

"And talk?" he asked.

"Talk is good."

I switched on the radio, a late-night talk show about the use of classic literature in schools. God knows how I'd found that show, and with a deft touch on the button, I switched to a 90s music channel, and we drove back to the pool house to everything from Justin Timberlake to Madonna. I parked, locked the car, and the two of us headed to my home away from home.

I wondered how long the talking would take and

whether this was the end of things. Shoulders back, determined to make my case, I slipped off my suit jacket and put it over the back of the nearest chair.

"I need to kiss you," he said and prodded me back against the wall, where he pinned me. "I don't want to talk."

The kiss was electric. The fact that we ended up on the floor of my hallway kissing and getting each other off was something else altogether.

This might have been a goodbye, but God, it was a hot goodbye. Lying spent in each other's arms on the hard floor, I waited for the words I dreaded.

"Seb?"

I carded my fingers through his soft hair. "Uh-huh?"

"You can say no if you don't want to, but I kind of have something to ask you."

THIRTEEN

Alex

His expression morphed from sated to tense, then to something harder to read.

"Can I get up before you ask this question? My back isn't too keen on this hard floor."

"Sure, yeah." I jumped up, tucked my dick back into my pants, and offered him a hand. The clean one, not the one coated with tacky jizz. "I need to…" I held up my hand and nodded at it. He did the same, a weak smile playing on his puffy lips. It thrilled me a bit to see that my kisses had made his lips so pink. That was probably a bad thing, but there it was.

We padded into the kitchen, washed up, and tried to get our clothes back into order. I'd ditched my jacket, tie, and shirt when we'd been pawing each other. Sebastian's gaze kept drifting to my chest and stomach as we dried our hands on some paper towels. Now that we'd burned off the lust, the air around us was thick and cumbersome.

"Coffee?" Seb asked, and I nodded. "You can ask what you wanted to ask while I get the kettle on. I went out and actually bought myself a kettle." He shook it at me as if to prove he'd gotten one. "I can't believe there was no electric kettle in this kitchen. And tea. I bought in tea, PG Tips tea from World Market. I take them everywhere with me. The other day I went to the coffee shop across from the arena and asked for tea, and they gave it to me black, and when I asked for a jug of milk, they brought me over an entire jug that held about a gallon in milk. Imagine a country where there are only a few kinds of tea to be had, but eight hundred and four brands of coffee. Heathens."

I chuckled at his nervous banter about tea, for goodness sake. Next thing, he'd be off about the weather, which was his other go-to subject whenever he was filling holes in a conversation. "I'm sorry if I'm making you uncomfortable."

He looked back at me as he filled the kettle with water. "It's not so much that I'm uncomfortable. Well, perhaps things are a *bit* awkward, but it's more a sensation of being hurled one way, then heaved the other. I'm not sure, but I'm suffering a slight whiplash."

"Yeah, I know." I shoved my hands into my front pockets, fingering the change and the edge of my cell phone. "I'm sorry for that too. My head has been... well, it's been a mess for a long time. Meeting you has made it messier."

He sighed heavily, then turned to face me, kettle in hand. "I never meant to make your life harder, Alex."

"No, hey, no. I didn't mean that in a bad way. Well." I flipped over a quarter in my pocket. "Okay, in a bad way maybe just a little, but that bad way led to a good way."

His sleek eyebrow skittered up his forehead. "You have thoroughly lost me."

"I figured." He gave me a tired sort of smile, then turned to place the kettle on.

"Can we sit down? Maybe I can get my thoughts aligned better if I'm not looking at your ass."

He shook that tight ass for me. That made me laugh, and some of the tension riding the cool air currents faded.

"We'll sit, but you have to put a shirt on," he countered, so to make things fair, we sat on the couch after I pulled my shirt on. I didn't button it, though. I loved his eyes roaming over my body almost as much as I loved his hands doing the same.

"Okay, so here's the thing…" I wiggled around to face him, one leg drawn up, my arm on the back of the couch, my fingers resting on his shoulder. "Today two things happened. And from the outside, they might not seem like big things, but, for me they were monumental."

He nodded at me to continue. I slid my finger under the collar of his shirt just for the tactile. His skin was warm, soft, and scented like a summery citrus drink. I could taste it forever.

"When we were leaving the dressing room, Louis Dillinger found me. Louis and I played on the same college team. He now plays for LA," I explained to ease that confusion on his face. "We were pretty close back in the day. Always dated together, that sort of thing. Anyway, tonight he texted me. Louis is a great guy. Real ladies' man. So he invited me to his hotel room where he said there were twins waiting for us."

Sebastian's eyes widened just a bit. "That's quite the friendly offer."

"Right? And at one time, like maybe six months ago, I would have done it. I would have gone with him back to his hotel, and I would have banged one of them because *soy un hombre macho.*" I clapped my chest. "I'm a macho man," I translated and got a bob of his head. "I had to prove it to everyone. Tonight, I said no thanks. I told him I had someone special and that I wanted to be with them."

His eyes lit up. "That's sweet. I think you're special as well."

I brushed the back of my fingers over his collarbone. "I really like you a lot. So much." I sighed when he leaned in to brush a kiss over my lips. "Right, so, back to the stuff, or we'll be lying on the floor again." He snorted softly. "I felt good about turning him down, like it was another small step in putting distance between the real Alejandro and this huge fake-ass persona that I've been pretending to be. As I was walking down the hall, feeling all cocky about my progress, I realized that I'd not said I had a special guy at home. That ate at me a little."

"Alex, there's no right or wrong way to proceed down the path of self-enlightenment and acceptance. Every small step leads us in the right direction." The kettle switched off and he stood and went to tend to the drinks. When he returned, he passed me a cup of his weird-ass instant coffee, then settled down beside me with a cup of tea cradled in his hands.

"Thanks, this smells good." I lied, then took a sip, and smiled, before resting the big blue mug on my thigh, where it warmed my leg nicely. "So anyway, I was upset about not being gayer or something, I don't know."

"I think you're plenty gay." He winked and pulled down his collar to show me a fresh love mark on his clavicle.

"Hashtag sorry not sorry." His eyes rolled. "There I was, wondering how I could be gayer and not come out when my phone rang. It was my little sister, Elizabeth. She was calling to tell me that she'd stood up to *Mamá* and *Abuela* and picked the boy she wanted to be her *chambelán de honor*. She was giddy with pride and ran on and on about this boy Dwayne, who not only is *not* Latino but black; he's not even Catholic. She and he are flirty dating, according to her. I have no idea what flirty dating is, but she's met his family, and they love her."

"Good on her," he replied, sipping his tea and patiently waiting for me to get to the damn point.

"Yeah, I said the same thing. Her choice was not a popular one in my house, and she's taking a lot of flack from the older folks, but she's sticking to her guns. She's so strong, so sure of herself, so powerful. And then there's me. I'm older than she is, bigger, stronger, and yet she makes me look like a mouse. It shames me that my little sister has more backbone than I do. What kind of man hides from his truth?"

"Alex…"

"I want you to come with me to my sister's *quinceañera*, as my date."

He looked as if someone had slugged him in the solar plexus. His eyes flared, his mouth parted a bit, and his cup of tea sat on his lower lip frozen in place. He lowered his mug, wet his lips, and blinked.

"I don't know what a *quinceañera* is, I'm sorry."

"Oh, no, don't be sorry. It's a party. Um, kind of like a sweet sixteen party or a debutante ball?" He nodded. "It's a celebration of a girl turning fifteen and signals her becoming a woman. It is a huge deal in the Latino culture. Everyone dresses formally, and my parents are going to spend a fortune on it."

He stared at me dully, as if his mind was having trouble with the whole concept. "And you want to take me to this highly important celebration as your date?"

"Yes."

He slowly placed his mug of tea on the table, then twisted around to look me right in the eye. "Alex, I'm not sure this is the best way for you to come out."

"I'll tell my family before the *misa de acción de gracias*." Again, the lost expression. "It's a mass of thanksgiving for the girl who is making the transition to a young woman."

"There's a mass?"

"Oh yes. Trust me, there's a mass for everything. Broken toenails get an hour of devotions."

"Ah, well, this is…"

"I get it if you don't want to be part of all the shit that's going to go down. I understand totally. I'll be happy to go stag, but I'm going to tell my family that I'm gay. I can't go on like this anymore. The fear, the worry, the constant terror of someone finding out is killing me. It's ruining my game; it's stripping all the joy out of my life. If they hate me, then they hate me, fine. I'll at least be free to be me."

He slid his hand up along my jaw, his palm still toasty warm from his tea. "I would be honored to go to Elizabeth's *quinceañera* as your date."

"Yeah?" A million suns flared to life in my chest.

"Oh yes."

"I think I love you."

"The feeling is mutual."

We kissed for so long our drinks went cold. Which was fine. I dug iced coffee, and I *really* dug him.

THE NEXT DAY, bright and early, still full of excitement and self-determination, I went to visit Henry. Ryker had some sort of team photo shoot that Sebastian had set up, and had to attend, something at a local shelter with puppies, so I winged it solo. The ride was cool, the blistering sun just starting to warm the dry air. I stopped for a breakfast sandwich and extra-large coffees for me and Henry, got some gas, and then rolled to the rehab center with Maluma and Ricky Be-Still-My-Fucking-Heart Martin blaring out of my speakers. Man, I had it bad for Ricky, but who didn't? Guess I'd been a fan of older men for longer than I realized. I grinned as I thought of a saying my *abuela* liked to toss around when talking about Mr. Martin. She'd say, "*Ricky Martin es como una pasa. Cuantas más arrugas más sabrosa es la fruta.*"

I couldn't argue. Ricky *was* like a raisin. The more wrinkles, the tastier the fruit was dead on, kind of like Sebastian. Not that my guy had lots of wrinkles, but he had some beautiful fine lines by his eyes and mouth. Life and laughter lines. Sexy-as-hell lines that I liked to pepper with soft kisses when we cuddled. Grinning and humming, I whipped into the rehab center's parking lot with *No Se Me Quita* filling the morning air. Then *he* stepped out of the wide double doors, and all those good feelings disappeared like fog over a lake once the sun crests the horizon.

"Hey, Speedy Gonzales, we have a speed limit here!"
Mr. Rent-A-Cop shouted as he stalked over to glare at
me. "Slow the hell down and turn that shit off. We have
sick people trying to recuperate, and your loud ethnic
music is disturbing the peace these patients require."

I cranked off the engine, and the music died away.
He stood right on the other side of the driver's side door,
a big man for sure, but not big enough to intimidate me.
I was probably twenty years younger than he was, a
professional athlete, and a damn good fighter. If he
wanted to bring it, I'd bring it. I should have confronted
the *idiota racista* the last time he'd given me shit, but I'd
been a good Latino boy.

"Right, but you standing here shouting at the top of
your lungs isn't disturbing the patients?" I fired back.
His nostrils flared.

"Are you mouthing back at me?"

"No, sir, I'm just pointing out that your raised voice
is probably more upsetting than a lively song about the
beauty of this man's lover's kiss on his mouth."

His hand came to rest on his handgun. That sealed
my flapping gums quickly, which was just what the
asshole wanted. He leaned over the door, making me
wish I had the roof on my Jeep. His blue eyes were
narrow, his thin blond hair whipped in the wind, and his
lips had a hateful smile on them.

"You seem like a punk to me. A little beaner punk
who thinks he's above the rules and regulations because
he plays hockey on some loser team. Let me tell you
something, and I want you to listen closely, *amigo*. The
next time you give me lip is the last time you're allowed
on these premises. I will haul your greasy ass out of this
car and perform a citizen's arrest for speeding in an area

marked fifteen miles per hour. I may also have witnessed a felony of some sort now that I think about it. Maybe you're sneaking illegal substances into this facility. Better let me check that bag of food there, in case it's full of drugs your mother snuck across the border."

It took every ounce of willpower I possessed not to punch him in the face and instead to reach slowly for the white bag on the seat next to me and pass it over to him. Peter Marks, that was the name on his tag, opened the bag, peeked inside, looked at me, and then walked off, making a pointed show of shoving the food I had bought for Henry into a trash can before he went inside.

Ten minutes I sat there, hands rolled into fists, shaking with rage until I had calmed myself enough that I thought I might be able to go see Henry and smile at one of my best friends. Peter sat just inside the door, talking amiably to a couple of people, smiling and joshing, his gaze darting to me as I strolled around them, coffee cups in my hand. I gave him a blank look and went about my business. I did not want to be the next person of color shot in the back by some idiot bigot with a gun and a hatred of *others*, even though I was as much an American citizen as he was.

Henry was propped up in his bed, surrounded by flowers, looking wan and unhappy when I arrived. His face lit up a bit when he saw me. I gave him a gentle hug of sorts, then sat next to the bed, handing him his caramel cloud macchiato while I took a tentative sip of my caffè americano.

"Ah, thanks, I miss these," he said, then fumbled to try to pry the plastic lid off. I sat up and helped him out, settling back into my seat once he'd had a sip. "I miss so much. I'm starting to think I'll never get out of here."

His eye was still patched, his leg casted, and his mood low. "You'll be out of here in no time and back on the ice by next season. No, man, don't argue with me. I got amazing mental powers. I can predict the future by reading the foam in my coffee cup."

"You don't drink coffee with foam," he quickly pointed out. I snickered. "It's good to see you, Alex. My parents come as often as they can, and my brother. Mom is saying I'm going to need to go home to their place back in Illinois to continue my therapy once they boot me from here. I do *not* want to move back to Wheaton, but the doctors say I can't be by myself and will need someone to stay with me."

"Move back in with me and Ry. We'll keep an eye on you." I pushed aside a huge floral arrangement. The card had *Adler* scribbled on it, tucked in among the vibrant pink and purple flowers.

He shook his head. "You guys are taking off as soon as the season ends. Ryker to Minnesota and Jacob, and you back to San Luis with your family."

"No way. I'll stay here and take care of you." I glanced around the room. "Like, does Adler Lockhart send flowers every day?" Each spare inch was thick with flowers, all with that white card with the chicken scratch signature.

"Yeah. So far, he's also sent me an Apple watch, a new phone, fourteen pens, a jar of pickled beets, and a kitten."

My eyes rounded. That made Henry smile. Gosh, he was cute when he smiled. "A real kitten?"

"Well, no, a stuffed one with a certificate to some no-kill shelter outside of Harrisburg, saying a kitten adoption had been arranged for me once I was discharged."

"Dude has a serious gift-giving thing," I murmured.

"I guess so. I would like a kitten, though. Summer is going to be long, and my parents and me… we have moments where we don't get along."

"Maybe Lockhart can find you someone to stay with you over the summer while you recuperate and do your therapy here in Arizona," I offered, and he nodded slowly as if giving that some serious thought. Then his stomach rumbled, as did mine, and I bitched at Pete *Dickhead* Marks inside my head. No reason to upset Henry with that shit; he had enough on his plate. "I better get going, morning skate. Coach is a sphincter about being late."

"Yeah, I recall. Tell everyone I said hi, and thanks for this." He held up his coffee. "I miss this, and you, and just doing normal stuff like stopping for breakfast or hanging out watching scary movies. My life… it kind of sucks."

Shit.

"It's going to get better, I promise." I stood, patted his thigh gently, and touched his fist with mine. Pete and I had a visual showdown at the front doors, but he never left his seat. Guess the shithead had cowed me enough earlier. I slid behind the wheel of my Jeep, kissed two fingers, and placed them to the small statue of the Blessed Virgin dashboard statue. She had been with me since I had bought my first car, a gift from my mother. "Please watch over Henry. *Santa María, madre de Dios.*"

I backed up slowly, eased past the doors, and then cranked up *Abuela's* favorite Spanish radio station, the one that played traditional Mexican songs. *Guadalajara* blasting, I flew over the last speed bump and out into the street, the sounds of a mariachi band flowing behind me. In my rearview, I caught the sight of Pete the Dickhead running outside to glower at me. I laughed all the way to the barn.

FOURTEEN

Seb

"AND THE POINT IS?" Colorado asked, his hands on his hips, his chin jutted, and I knew that getting him on the Zamboni was going to be an exercise in futility unless I sweetened the deal. Still, I'd try the hard way first because sometimes Colorado let me win.

"The point is that we film you and Alex racing the Zambonis from here to there." I waved at the finish line down at the other end of the parking lot at the Raptors practice facility. "You'll be mic'd up, viewers will hear what you are saying, and laugh, and it will all be wonderful promotion for the team."

He scowled, and then he got a calculating look in his eye. Shit, there it was, the goalie's art of making a deal coming to the surface. I hadn't had an issue with Alex, who was already sitting on his Zamboni, staring at the finish line and visualizing the course if I knew him.

"I'll do this if you get me out of the GoPro thing."

I sighed inwardly. GoPros were cameras that were affixed to the helmets. The player would go off and do his thing on the ice, and the GoPro would feed back what he was looking at. I'd earmarked Ryker and Colorado both to do the event after free practice tomorrow, and I couldn't understand why any of these cocky hockey players wouldn't want to show off their skills.

"GoPro," I repeated.

"Yep, shit makes me dizzy when I watch it back after." He tilted his head as if daring me to argue.

I paused for a long moment as if I was considering the issue. "Have you thought of not watching it?" I asked.

He looked incredulous and pointed his thumbs at his chest. "Have you seen me? Who wouldn't want to watch it?"

Marcia, the camera operator, cleared her throat. "Guys, I need to get out of here on time today."

A few more moments of pretending to think and then I gave a grudging sigh. "Okay, we have a deal."

He let out a whoop and then clambered up on top of his Zamboni and patted it. "Model five hundred," he said. "Did you know that this machine's top speed is nine-point-seven mph and can go from zero to a quarter mile in ninety-three-point-five seconds?" He patted it again, then settled in the seat. "Prepare to be slaughtered, Cherry," he shouted over to Alex. For some reason he'd started calling Alex Cherry Garcia, and the cherry part had stayed. I'd noticed a few people in the locker room had taken to calling Alex that, and I think he was cool with it and was even a little bit proud. I could see that to get your official hockey nickname was a highlight of a skater's career.

"Okay, let's do this," Marcia confirmed, and after a few mic tests for audio, we were ready to go. I'd even found a checkered flag on the web and carefully taped it together with a Raptors logo, and it was me who was starting this. Marcia counted us in.

"Gentlemen, start your engines."

Alex fumbled the start, which had Colorado shouting something at him, both of them in fits of hysterics before they even started. It did my heart good to see Alex laughing because as we grew closer to his sister's fifteenth party, he was getting more and more jumpy. Not on the ice, no, on the ice, he was a bloody genius, taking chances, using his body, and the JAR line was getting things done. On top of that, the social media campaign was bringing interest, particularly when I handed the Twitter account to a young intern from UA. He was a funny guy, made jokes, entered into Twitter discussions with other teams, and had created an entire one-upmanship type battle with the team from LA. The optics were good, and there was an entire growing fan base for both Ryker and Alex. People were focusing less on the fact that the team was sucking, and began to call it rebuilding. Added to that were some limited successes on the ice, some wins, a couple of points from end of normal time ties, and the fact that Aarni's countersuit had been rejected as having no grounds.

But it was Alex I was watching now as he and Colorado snaked their way through two identical courses next to each other, Colorado only slightly ahead at one of the wide and almost impossible-to-achieve turns around cones. They were trash-talking, whooping loudly, and Marcia was getting it all, even the bits where Colorado hung dangerously over the side as if he was riding a horse.

I loved Alex to the point he and the team were all I had the capacity to think about. The ten years between us didn't matter, and the fact that he was a newbie to the entire sex-with-guys thing had never been an issue. I'd never been with anyone who was as responsive as Alex, and I doubted I ever would.

Of course, our time was limited. I knew that, but I was concentrating on the here and now and enjoying the warmth and happiness of being *in love*.

Alex had edged ahead of Colorado now after the goalie had done some kind of booty dance and gotten distracted, and even though I had to remain impartial and this was just a stupid publicity stunt, I was so damn proud of my man out there winning.

Yeah, I had it that bad.

I jogged down the course with the flag as they wound in and out of the cones, Alex flattening two of them, and then I waved it as the two of them approached the finish line. I sensed that Marcia was zooming in on Alex's wide grin, capturing Colorado's bellowing laugh, and when they passed the flag, it was Alex who'd won.

Marcia moved closer to capture the post-race interviews, and I could hear the guys chirping at each other from here.

"Cherry blatantly ran over cones." Colorado was faking outrage. "I want this entire cheating debacle sent up for video review."

"Yeah, yeah, whatever, loser. You're just sore that I beat you so badly."

Cue the two of them roughhousing, giggling, and shouting like idiots. Then it was a wrap, and it would be up to me to edit everything, along with the documentary company that was close to having episode two of the Raptors series in the bag. If we could win tomorrow against Dallas, then that would be the perfect end to the VT, and I think the feeling of hope was infectious in the entire building. Tonight was our first rental of the old events room. A local company, Catalina Foothills Chrysler Plymouth, one of our sponsors, had hired it for a fiftieth birthday party. That was where I needed to be next, talking to one of the owners, Robert Lake, confirming menus, taking photos, updating the website with the media team, and I really needed our intern to get some tweets with excerpts of the Zamboni race up on the Net.

"Earth to See-bast-i-yan." Colorado waved a hand in front of my face.

"Sorry?" I asked as I snapped back to the present.

"You lot apologize all the time," he commented.

"Sorry?" I realized what I'd done. "My lot?" I then added and raised an eyebrow.

"Yeah, you sexy Hugh Grant types."

Oh, it was the English thing again. I smiled at Colorado, which maybe I shouldn't have done.

"I fucked this English guy once," Colorado confided. "He was all Prince William vowels and *Downton Abbey* politeness, and one of the best one-night stands I ever had." He ended the sentence with a laugh as if it was a joke, but there was no laughter in his eyes.

I blinked at him, not entirely sure I was hearing right. What the hell was that? Alex was with Marcia over at the other side of the parking, giving an interview, and it was just me and Colorado. Was he sharing a joke, or was it personal? Did he want me to respond to the emptiness in his eyes? He struck me as such a positive upbeat man who didn't take shit from everyone, but something was off with him.

"Are you all right?" I asked.

"Of course." He punched my arm before ambling off to join Alex, me following. God knows what all that was about.

"That was so cool," Alex announced as he and Colorado bumped fists, then did a complicated bro hug before separating.

"Later, guys." I sketched a wave and left them to it.

I didn't have to be an expert to know that someone was following me, and Alex caught up with me at the side door. He was very close to me as we went down the quiet corridor, and I wasn't surprised when he tugged me into an even darker passage that smelled of antiseptic. He stole the first kiss before I was ready for it, and I stumbled back to hit the wall with him sprawled over me. The kiss deepened as soon as I was steady, and he carded his fingers through my hair before linking his hands behind my neck. I didn't care who walked past us at this moment. All I wanted was to hold him close and never stop kissing him.

Only I couldn't. We had work to do, or at least I had to get back to my office, and Alex needed to get himself off to do whatever he did post-free practice and a Zamboni race. Probably conditioning or something so that his sexy body was even harder. Just the thought of that had any of my remaining blood heading south to join the rest.

"Hi," he said as he pulled away and rearranged his jersey.

"Hi, back," I copied, but it was a lot harder to hide an erection in suit pants and a shirt.

"Did you see me win?" he asked and ran a hand over my covered cock.

I removed his hand from me. "Not helping," I whispered, wishing he'd ignore me and maybe do some more touching. Instead, he winked.

"I know. But you love me, so it's okay."

We'd said those words to each other so many times, and they never grew old.

"I guess I do," I said and smiled at him in the gloom.

He gave me one last hard kiss, and then he was gone, and I was left waiting until I could leave without causing offense to everyone I passed.

"You need to look after him." Colorado's voice shocked the hell out of me, which was the best cure for being turned on, ever.

"Pardon me?" I asked, ever so politely.

"His secret is worse than the rest of us, you know, with his family and religion. Yeah?"

"I know." I moved out of the shadows, and Colorado stared at me with an expression I'd seen when the camera zoomed in on him in net—focused intensity. He clapped me on the shoulder.

"You're one of the good ones, Prince Will."

I didn't even have to ask if I'd just been gifted a Colorado-approved nickname, I just knew that is what he would call me from now on. Bastard.

Although if I was honest, I actually liked it.

FIFTEEN

Alex
_____

THE TEAM SLOGGED through the rest of March, and the end of the season was just five games away. We were going to end the year in fourth place in our division of eight teams, more than likely. Which was a slot higher than last year but still not great. Coach had given me a pass on the game tomorrow after I'd explained how important this family event was. Ever since that talk with him, my respect for Coach Carmichael had grown. He was firm, yes, and sometimes strict, but he had a good heart and a love of hockey that made us all want to do better for him. And I did love hockey. It was my ticket to great things and had led me to wonderful places.

What had my full attention now was my bold plan to come out to my family. My sister's party was tomorrow, and as we drove to San Luis, flashes of upcoming horrors played out in my mind. This was not going to be pretty. Not at all. My gut was a tight knot, but my resolve was strong. Having Sebastian at my side helped. He was a calming influence. His personality was laid back, slow to anger, pleasant, and polite to the point where I wanted to kick his ass at times. Whereas I was mostly his opposite. Although I did try to be kind and courteous, I did tend to run hot. We balanced each other.

I glanced over at him and smiled. He was such a desert rat now. Shades, loose cotton shirt, tan shorts, and leather sandals. His hair was starting to lighten up as his skin began to darken. He was still several shades of pale in comparison to me, but that was just another thing that I loved about us. Lying in bed naked next to him, his skin creamy white and mine copper, our love was a thing of beauty that flew past stupid biases or bigotry. Age, gender, race. None of that mattered when two hearts were joined. I prayed my family would see that as well.

"You should watch the road," he pointed out. I quickly veered back into my lane. "Good lad."

"We're going to be reaching San Luis in about ten minutes," I said, then reached up to turn down one of my favorite Thalía songs. "You still have time to change your mind."

"Not a chance. You're stuck with me."

I grinned, but the joy was a false one. By the time I pulled into the driveway of my parents' modest home, my nerves were shot. As the engine cooled, I sat there staring at the house where I'd grown up, too scared to get out of my Jeep.

"I'll be right beside you," Sebastian said, his voice easing me from the gaping maw of panic I'd been staring at.

"Okay, yeah, so let's do this."

As soon as the front door creaked open, smells, sounds, and siblings assaulted me. Several cousins, aunts, and a couple of uncles as well. Sebastian snuck in behind me, smiling politely as my baby sister threw herself at me. I made quick introductions, Elizabeth's intelligent brown eyes jumping from Sebastian, whom I said was my friend, to me. She linked her arms through ours and bulled her way forward.

Kids from crawling age to teens milled around, patting my back as I waded through my huge and gregarious family. I found my mother and grandmother in the kitchen, cooking for tonight's dinner.

"*Mamá,* look who finally made it!" Elizabeth shouted, then shoved me into the group of women packed into the small kitchen. I glanced back as I was pinched, kissed, patted, and had spoons laden with flavorful beef, pork, and chicken pushed at me. I hugged my mother hard as I chewed one of *Abuela's* stuffed peppers.

"*Mi niño!*" *Mamá* cooed as she pushed my hair from my face. "*Deberías habertelo cortado para la fiesta, Alejandro.*"

"It's fine." I sighed, looking over my mother's head to find Elizabeth and Sebastian in a rather deep discussion over by the back door. "It's just the right length for the party. *Abuela,* tell her it's a good look on me."

My grandmother came to my defense, as she always had. Soon the room was alive with Spanish that flowed out the open windows. I wiggled free after being fussed over and pulled Sebastian out of the corner.

"This is Sebastian," I called, and about twenty pairs of judgmental brown eyes zeroed in on us. "He's my good friend."

The silence was deafening. The happy chatter of

Spanish women died off. My mother whispered something that I couldn't quite catch.

"Pleasure to meet you all," Seb said as the uneasy feeling intensified.

Not knowing exactly what had set them off, I nudged Sebastian out of the back door. We fell out of estrogen land right into testosterone world. The looks that my father, uncles, and cousins tossed at us made me wonder if the ugly silence in the kitchen wasn't better. The guys were seated under the shade trees, watching a baseball game. I made the introductions. Seb was never going to be able to recall all the names, poor guy.

"Alejandro, come have a beer," my cousin Héctor called from the picnic table where the TV had been placed. "The women chased us out." He slapped my back, then gave Seb a funny, drunken look. I fished a cold beer out of the cooler, handed one to Seb, and dropped down in the shade, my legs straddling the wooden bench, Sebastian seated right beside me.

The cloud of uncertainty began to envelop us as we spent thirty minutes or so watching the game.

"So, Alejandro, I thought perhaps you'd come home with a pretty girl, not some white foreigner," Héctor slurred, his gaze lingering on Sebastian as he flung out that rather pointed comment. "Surely there are enough women for you to pick from that you don't have to haul this Anglo asshole around? Unless your time playing with that Madsen fag has rubbed off?"

This was all said in Spanish. Sebastian glanced at me as I stewed on how to reply. My father began chiding Héctor, but he was the only one speaking up. Damn it. I'd not even gotten to see my older brother and sister, as they were still working.

"*Alex…*" Sebastian whispered as the tension thickened.

"No, actually, playing with Ryker didn't rub off. I was a fag long before I ever skated with him."

"Oh fuck no! This asshole turned you?" Héctor roared, his face mottled with an insane and instant fury.

Things kind of went from bad to motherfucking horrible in the blink of an eye. For some reason, Héctor took a swing at Sebastian, who had no idea what was going on as the only language being spoken was Spanish. The shot caught Seb in the eye, and I went over the picnic table, jumped on my aunt's son, and began beating on him. Chairs and drinks went flying as men joined the melee.

When my father finally had me subdued and pinned to the high wooden fence around our yard, Héctor was being helped inside, his face a bloody mess. Sebastian had been given some ice in a bag and was sitting in a lawn chair, ice on the right side of his face, his head down nearly between his knees. So many people were yelling at me all at once that I couldn't understand anything being said. The few things I did understand was my baby sister was crying over by the table that held the boxes of yellow custom printed T-shirts for the party tomorrow, all of which had been knocked to the ground and trampled, my mother was ashen and shaken, and my *abuela* was fingering her rosary while patting Sebastian on the back.

I jerked free of my father, no easy task, and hurried over to kneel in the grass beside Sebastian. My knee landed in some spilled beer. He lifted his head. I was stunned to see a wobbly sort of smile on his handsome face.

"Your family certainly knows how to throw a bash."
He chuckled, then moaned. I rested my brow on his
thigh. Somewhere in the foggy distance, I could hear my
father herding people out of the house. Seb ran his
fingers through my hair. "My hero," he whispered as the
extended family vacated the premises. When it was just
my grandmother, my mother, my father, and my sister, I
stood, my fingers resting on Seb's shoulder.

"I'm sorry this happened this way," I said shakily, my
knuckles weeping blood. They all stared at me in
obvious shock, well, except for *Abuela*, who nodded as if
this were something she'd been expecting. "I'd meant to
tell you over dinner when it was just us, but fucking
Héctor—"

"Alejandro, watch your mouth," *Papá* snapped. I
murmured an apology. "We're quite upset at you for
doing this!"

"Yes, why did you have to ruin your sister's big day?"
Mamá asked, and I had no real answer for her. "What
did you do to make this happen? *How* did this happen?
Did I not raise you right?"

"*Mamá*, stop it!" Elizabeth snarled, using her long
sleeves to swipe at her eyes. "You're making it sound like
Alejandro being gay is dirty and wrong! It's not."

"In the eyes of God—"

"No, *Mamá*, God loves all his children," Elizabeth
argued. I loved my feisty little sister so much. "This kind
of shit is insane and why our world is so full of hate!
Anyone who's a little different is wrong and sinful.
That's bullshit! You don't like Dwayne because he's
black, and now you don't like your own son because he's
gay? That's stupid, and *you're* stupid!"

"*Elizabeth!*" *Papá* shouted, but she would not be

quieted, not until my father threatened to cut off her allowance. Then and only then did she sit down. Not by them, but next to Sebastian.

"Can we all please stop yelling and talk to poor Alejandro?" *Abuela* enquired, tottering around to find a soft seat in the shade. "Such a big shout about such a small thing."

"The boy being a gay is not a small thing!" my mother barked, then lowered her voice in case the neighbors were eavesdropping. I suspected it was far too late to worry about the Santos-Garcia disgrace leaking out. The whole block knew I'd announced I was gay and had beaten up my cousin. I'd do it again. No one took a swing at my boyfriend. Not as long as I was still sucking air.

"Yes, it is. He's been so for a long time, and there is no wrong in it. How can love be wrong?" *Abuela* asked, then picked up someone's beer and took a long pull from the bottle. "Such going on about who kisses whom. Your aunt Celeste was gay too, but you do not see me yelling at her."

"*Tia* Celeste has been dead for twenty years," I explained to Seb, who nodded, then grimaced. "Look, I know this has been bad. We can go. I think we should go."

"Yes, I think you should," my mother whispered, her eyes wet with tears.

Elizabeth began shouting again, my grandmother did as well, but in the end, I took Sebastian by the hand and led him back to my Jeep. My baby sister followed us.

"Stay please, stay," she begged, her smooth cheeks damp. I pulled her into my chest and hugged her hard, long strands of her dark hair blowing into my face.

"Please, don't let them drive you off. Stay. We'll talk it out. Please, please, I want you there. It's *my* fucking party, not theirs! Please, stay? Don't let assholes like Héctor ruin things for you. Please, please, stay."

I threw a look at Seb, who was standing by my Jeep, his eye swollen and already turning a nice shade of black. I was going to kill Héctor.

"Should we stay? It's up to you, Sebastian."

SIXTEEN

Seb

ALEX's *abuela* bustled toward us, looking as if she was on a mission, and I even took a step back to avoid her walking into me.

"We talk," she said.

Next to me, Alex shook his head. "I don't want you in the middle of this, *Abuela*."

I thought maybe it would be good to have a mediator, but it seemed as if she had certain ideas about me and Alex.

"Come, come, sit down. I have sage advice to pass you." She tugged my arm to separate me from Alex, and I sent him a worried glance. He closed his eyes briefly and then shook his head, so I followed her to the bench.

"Now, first I say this for you to hear. *Mi nieto*, my grandson, for many years thinks he is clever in his fooling." She tapped her chest. "But me, I see all with Alejandro. I know for long times he is gay. My sister Celeste was *lesbiana*, ever since she was old enough to know boy from girl. Back in my youth days, people did not come out with big prides like they do now. Being a lesbian would be the ultimate insult to any man, being an 'inferior being who doesn't give me what she should'." Pain stabbed my chest, and she looked devastated as she spoke. I was being included in some great truth here and the weight of it was suffocating. "Celeste's sweetheart, she suffered so, from every kind of corrective rape, she was forced to marry to avoid scandal, only when her husband died was she released and found Celeste. *Homosexuales* and the *lesbianas*, they hide. Always hiding for fear of bad feelings from family and church." She shook her head and paused.

"I'm sorry," I murmured.

She patted my knee. I wasn't sure if it was to reassure me or to ground herself. "Celeste, she never say any words about her true self to our parents. She hid herself from them, but she tell me. She tell me out of eight other sisters. And I tell her to be honest, always. Tell *Mamá* and *Papá*, but she would not do it. She died, never telling her truth. She died alone, with no love for too many years." She pressed a hand to her chest. "This breaks my heart. God does not say anyone is bad for loving who they love; only the people say this." She spoke passionately.

"I agree," I said. "So the advice you're giving me is what? To help Alex see that—"

"No, not just that. You are older man than Alejandro, more settled in life. Living more, you see more. You must go talk to my daughter. Make her see that they may lose their son if they do not try to make a come together, *un compromiso. Sí?* Do you understand, Sebastian?"

I did understand. But the thought of finding Alex's parents and talking to them was terrifying. I was already the bad guy, the one whom Héctor had accused of turning their son. Or was that Elonso? I couldn't recall properly, because my head hurt, and my thoughts were spinning so fast I felt sick. When I'd first gone to Cambridge, the odd one out in the group of rich kids I'd been lumped in with, I decided there and then I would become something different, a brand-new person who spoke without an accent, who was clever and funny and could carry a conversation.

All I'd needed to do then was channel my inner bravery, and that was what I needed to find again. For Alex.

"I will," I said and stood, brushing the seat of my shorts and heading to the house.

"What are you doing?" Alex called.

"Give me some time," I said and watched Alex being blocked from following me by his *abuela* and a very determined Elizabeth. I hesitated by the side door, and then, shoulders back, I knocked sharply. I heard movement inside, and then Papa Garcia opened the door and peered out, probably checking for Alex. I could see the concern in his expression when he located his son out by the road.

"Now is not a good time," he said and went to close the door in my face, but I stopped the door shutting with my hand, and he didn't use any force to make me remove the block. If anything, there was a glint of respect in his eyes, and he sighed. "You'd better come in."

The door took me into a hallway, and he led me into the kitchen, where only a short while before Alex had been pinched and hugged and loved on by everyone, and where everyone had judged my being there. Now it was empty and silent, all apart from the soft breaths of Alex's mama, but it still smelled of tomato and herbs, and food was piled to one side. Everything had gone so wrong today, and with hindsight, maybe Alex should have spoken to his parents one-on-one well before entering a full house where anything could, and did, happen.

"Sir, ma'am, could we talk?" I didn't sit until I was asked, didn't move fully into the kitchen until his mama looked up at me and nodded. That was a good sign, right? All I knew was that the Catholic Church's position on homosexuality was based on a distinction between being lesbian or gay and acting on it, accepting the first part but clinging to the fact that acting on it was a sin and was wrong.

I stood by the table, and my chest was tight with nerves and pain. What would happen if I made things worse? What if I fucked things up for Alex and he lost his family and didn't want me. What would he do?

His mama was mumbling under her breath, her rosary in her hand, and her eyes were bloodshot. She'd been crying; that much was clear.

"Sit down," Papa Garcia ordered, and I did what he'd asked immediately. This was like going to the principal's office for a punishment, but that didn't mean I had to act as if I was scared and unable to talk.

"Why?" Mama Garcia said in an anguished tone.

Why what? Why had he told them? *Or* why was he even gay in the first place. He was born that way, and he wanted his family to know. That would answer everything but seemed so dismissive.

"I don't understand the question," I said finally.

"Why now, why here?" she asked.

"Why at all?" Papa Garcia said in an ominously dark tone.

I was not going down that tunnel of science versus God, so I chose my language carefully.

"He is embracing the way that God made him," I said, and that much was true. Alex believed in God, he had faith, and being gay wasn't throwing away all of that, and I knew firsthand the challenge to be true to oneself.

Mama Garcia inhaled and let out a stream of Spanish, which I had no chance of keeping up with.

"*No hablo español.* I'm sorry."

This set off another tirade, but this time in perfectly clear English. "He says he is with a man, that he is gay, and the man he says he loves cannot even speak our language."

"I'll learn." In fact, I'd already begun with a few words, but this wasn't where I wanted this to go. I needed to talk of a compromise for Alex, not make promises to his parents about what kind of man I could be for Alex if only they'd let me. I took a couple of calming breaths. Papa Garcia had taken the other seat, opposite me, and was staring at me so hard I was surprised I wasn't combusting under the glare.

"I understand you need to process things because the news Alex gave you has devastated you, but surely that isn't a weight to put on Alex's shoulders? Can you try to accept that he is being truthful with you and that him coming out isn't about you. It's about Alex himself and the fact that we are in love."

Papa Garcia tensed even more. "Who are you to

come into my house and tell us how to think!" he snapped.

Fuck, I guessed that is what I had been doing, and I reconsidered my direction again. Why Alex's *abuela* thought I had a hope in hell's chance of garnering any kind of compromise here I didn't know.

"Alex thinks he has done something wrong, and he doesn't want to feel that way——"

"Is he sure?" Mama Garcia interrupted my sincere sentence, and for a moment I couldn't process the words.

"Is he sure he's gay? Yes, he is."

Silent tears tracked down her face. "He will die of AIDS. Marie Alonso's son is *SIDA* ! HIV, you call it. Worse, he will burn in hell, and I will not be able to save him. My Alejandro will burn for eternity, and you sit and tell me that he knows he is gay? How can a boy who loves his God, and is a good Catholic"—she made the sign of the cross—"even begin to have this hate for himself inside him."

Well, shit, that was some heavy paragraph to throw at me. "He won't get HIV any more than you would," I finally settled on saying. "Focusing on telling someone how they could die doesn't celebrate them being alive. I mean, I could get run over by a bus tomorrow and——"

"Show some respect," Papa Garcia interrupted.

"Can I bring him in? Can we talk, the four of us? Because he is out there brokenhearted. He's lost everything, and right now is the easiest time to make him feel like the loneliest person in the world. I can't speak for Alex, but I know that he has been lost in all of this, scared of what he felt. Scared of you."

Mama Garcia stared at me, and her eyes widened. "Scared?"

"Scared, lonely, lost, and he's a grown man, but he needs his family, and the thought of not having your love will destroy him."

"I don't want to hurt him," Mama Garcia murmured and reached for her husband's hand. "But his soul, how can I begin to…" She began to cry again, and Papa Garcia scooted closer so he could stroke her hair. It was such an intimate moment, seeing their thirty years or more of marriage and love in one touch. I wanted that with Alex, and he wanted that with me. I racked my brains to think of what I could do here. Without his family, Alex really would be lost. I could tell them I'd walk away, but that wouldn't make Alex not gay.

"Can I tell you something that happened last week?" They turned to look at me. "I watched four men approach him after a game, fans in jerseys, all of them full of beer, who wanted to ask him about hockey. From the beginning, I didn't like it. They seemed almost menacing, but by the time I'd carefully moved closer, they had him pinned in a corner. Not so you'd notice, but he couldn't move them out of the way without making a fuss. He was very polite, but they were goading him, and not once did he lose his temper or focus. That's on you as parents. He might hate what is happening to him, but he has a backbone of steel, and the pride he has? Overwhelms me sometimes."

"He can be stubborn," Mama Garcia admitted and lifted her chin. "And he's always been a good son."

There was a glimmer of light from behind dark clouds in her words, and I ran with it. "He'll always *be* a good son—" I stopped when Papa Garcia cursed loudly and left the room. It seemed as though, even as Alex's mama began to listen, that his papa had dismissed everything out of hand. If I could just get one of his parents to compromise, I had hope for him.

"He's a wonderful man, and I love him more than life itself. He will always have me, whatever happens, but he would be a broken man if he loses his family."

Her hand went to her chest, and she pressed it over her heart. "You truly love him? As a man loves a woman…" She was abruptly flustered. "I don't know how to say it."

"I love him as one person loves another," I encouraged gently. "Wholly and completely, and when I go home, it will be hard, but we'll make it work."

We sat in silence for a moment.

"You won't have to see me tomorrow, but Elizabeth wants her brother at her party and at the church. Please don't shut him out and break his heart."

She hugged herself hard, and I waited with bated breath.

"I will see Alex in the morning," she whispered. "I need to talk to his *papá*, try and keep them apart and calm everything down." Then she cleared her throat. "Not you, though. It's too much."

I could accept that, although I doubted Alex would be happy, but his mama was compromising, and maybe Alex needed to do so as well for a while.

"Thank you," I said quietly. Then I let myself out the back door. Alex was waiting for me, fear on his face.

"She'll be okay," I exaggerated the hope I'd seen in her. "She wants you there tomorrow."

He closed his eyes briefly and nodded, and I left him

so he and his sister could talk privately. When he
climbed into the car, he looked exhausted, and I wanted
to touch him or hold him. I didn't do either. Instead I
started the engine and headed for our hotel.

Where I'd need to tell him the deal I'd struck with
his mom.

SEVENTEEN

Alex

"No, forget it."

Sebastian's sullen expression wasn't going to sway me, nor would the pleading gaze.

"Alejandro." He sighed, grabbing my attention as I paced our comfy hotel room like a caged puma. I'd only heard him use my Spanish name once before. I was always Alex or a tender endearment of some sort. Obviously, I'd worked through all that British patience and decorum.

"No. I brought you because I wanted to be seen with you. To let my family know that we're a couple, that I'm gay, and I am not ashamed of being gay any longer."

"I'd say you have successfully announced your queer status to the entire Santos-Garcia clan quite robustly if not eloquently." He was seated in a green armchair by the window, the air blowing the white-and-green curtains, his eye turning more purple by the minute. "Now that the bomb has been dropped, it's time to start sifting through the debris for survivors."

"Of which there are none." I dropped to the bed,

my legs growing weary. I'd been circling this room for over an hour, trying to work off some of the emotions threatening to drown me.

"Not true," he replied softly, tossing his ice bag to the nightstand. "Your sister and grandmother are firmly behind you."

"Wow, two out of what? Two hundred?"

"Those two are more than many young gays have," he reminded me. I groaned at the guilt, the anger simmering inside me cooling a little. "I hazard to say that many more will be accepting as well."

"Not my parents…"

He stood, walked over to the bed, and sat beside me. His hand slipped around my back, and the dam broke. There was no curbing the rushing river of pain. It swept over the top of the dam just as I feared it would. A raspy gasp and the tears were there. Seb pulled me to his side, settling my head to his shoulder, and let me weep until I was unable to cry any longer.

"Here," he whispered, passing me a small emerald box of tissues. I wiped and blew and coughed, shame heating my cheeks. *Papá* would've been so disgusted to see these tears. Real men did not cry. Of course, *Papá* was already sickened about his youngest son, so would a crying fit really make him hate me more?

"I shouldn't have come out to them," I said, my voice scratchy and thick. "I knew I shouldn't have done this. Deep down, I knew it. The lie wasn't that bad of a way to live."

"Alex, you know that lie was eating you from the inside out like battery acid." He ran his hand over my hair and the nape of my neck. "Hiding who you were was corroding every aspect of your life from hockey to your friendships to any possible relationship you wished to have. No, coming out was right. It was a life-saving measure. Your chosen delivery method may have been a bit... cataclysmic, but the intent was sound."

A gruff laugh-snort burbled out of me. "I blew the *mierda* out of things."

"Yes, yes, you did, but that was inevitable. We knew your news was going to upset people. We didn't know they'd be so quick to punch a perfectly innocent Englishman in the face, though."

I squeezed my eyes shut. "I am so sorry you got hurt. This whole mess is just a... mess. I've lost my family now." The pain was incredible.

"No, no, you haven't. You still have family that loves you. Your mother wants to meet with you in the morning. Go see her. Sit down and talk with her." His touch on my scalp was soothing. I never wanted it to stop.

"Not without you," I stated with as much force as I could muster, which wasn't much. I was drained.

"Yes, without me. My presence upsets them, your parents, and I can understand why. No, please, just stop defending me. I love that you're so protective, I truly do." He pressed a kiss to my ear, right at the top. "But I'm a grown man. I am able to handle some dislike, trust me. Right now, they need distance from the older man who, they may feel, led you into this gay lifestyle."

"That's bullshit, and you know it!" I snapped, my head leaving his shoulder as a new wave of anger appeared.

"We know it, but they don't. Alex, they know little to nothing of the LGBT experience, only what they've been taught by nuns and priests. It's up to you to educate them. Calmly, rationally, and with love. Your parents love you a great deal. I saw that. They'll come around—I can feel it."

"But I want you at the party. You're my boyfriend. It's not fair that everyone else gets to bring the person they love, but I don't." As soon as that left my mouth, I heard the whiny brat tone it carried. "Nope, don't say it. Life isn't fair." I sighed. He gave me a weary smile. "What will you do all day tomorrow alone? I just... fuck! I hate the idea of leaving you here."

"I'll be fine. I have books on my phone to read, work that I can do, TV, a bar, and room service." He slipped his hand into my hair, his nails gently scratching over my scalp. I shuddered with delight, like a puppy getting a belly rub. "I'll be fine. It's only for four hours, right?"

"Yeah, but still..."

We both startled when someone knocked on the door. I rose and pattered into the bathroom to wash my face, leaving Seb to deal with whomever was rapping away. When I exited the bath, my cheeks chilled from cold water, I stalled as my gaze landed on Juan standing next to Sebastian.

My older brother took one look at me, opened his arms, and called me over. I choked on the feelings balling up suddenly in my throat. I jogged around the bed and hugged my brother so tightly he wheeze-laughed.

"*Oh, hermanito, qué día has tenido,*" he murmured as we hugged it out. Yeah, it had been one hell of a day for his little brother. "Luisa and Elizabeth, along with *Abuela*, are bending our parents' ears, informing them that they need to lighten the hell up, step into the twenty-first century, and let you live your life as God has intended you to."

I loved my siblings so fucking much right now I was speechless. The three of us sat up until midnight talking, sipping beer from the minibar in the corner, and trying to work out how to handle Elizabeth's *quinceañera* festivities tomorrow. There were no easy answers, but I'd been coerced into leaving Sebastian behind for this affair but no others. That was to be explained to my parents, the priest, and anyone else who had issue with the new gay Alejandro.

Still, having that all worked out didn't help me sleep. I lay in bed next to Seb, listening to him breathing and staring at the dark gray suit that I'd packed for the party hanging over the bathroom door. Morning brought more angst as I gathered my suit and dress shoes after my shower and shave and kissed Sebastian goodbye. I hated, and I mean *hated*, seeing that hotel door close between us. The drive to my parents' modest three-bedroom, two-bathroom house on East Adobe Street was not a happy one. I parked in the short drive outside the stucco home and stared at it. I'd grown up here. Played in the carport, went to school two blocks over, ridden my bike up and down the sidewalks, slept in a bunk bed over my brother for years. I'd eaten and bathed here, prayed here, and sang songs with *Abuela* here as we baked *empanadas*, *conchas*, and *marranitos*. Right now, it felt nothing like home. It was just an old house built in the late '80s that lacked heart. That was because I'd been forced to leave my heart back in that hotel room.

The front door opened, and Elizabeth raced out, her hair already artfully done up, her tiara fastened to her head, her eyes shining, and her feet bare. The cutoff jean shorts and BTS tank top paired with the glittery tiara piled among thick ebony curls was quite the look. It made me smile. *She* made me smile. I was swept up in her joy, and before I knew it, was inside the house, suit slung over my shoulder, listening to her go on and on about her gown, it was yellow, her makeup, her Dwayne, her first pair of high heels that *Papá* would give her and her last baby doll that *Mamá* would gift her with. I did not begrudge her being a little self-centered. It was her day. Not mine. I'd resigned myself after talking with Juan and Seb that I would not allow my shit to dim my baby sister's special day. If someone got into my face or slung slurs, I was ignoring them. Four hours. I could deal with hate for four hours. I'd done it all my life.

Mamá stepped out of the kitchen, her hair also gathered up off her neck in a fancy, curly style. She was in her robe and slippers, but her good pearl earrings dangled from her earlobes.

"You're early," my mother said, reaching out to touch my arm. "We're just doing our hair. *Abuela* is in her bedroom with your *Tía* Margarita. Come and sit with me. We should talk, I think, with some coffee."

"*Si, Mamá.*"

We walked past a large statue of the Virgin Mary, my great-grandmother's rosary hanging from the Virgin's praying hands. I kissed my fingers, then placed them on Mary's soft blue robes, asking her in my head for her love and guidance as I talked with my mother. I sat in my customary seat, the one beside the doorway, and smiled shakily at my mother when she placed a cup of strong coffee in front of me. She was a short woman, plump, with eyes the same color and shape as mine, or mine were like hers, to be precise.

"*Mijo*," she began, then paused as she worked out what she wished to say. "Alejandro, your sister and your grandmother told me I should not talk about the church, but how can I not when so much of what we are is part of the church?"

"I think they mean not to use religion to hide behind. If you have a problem with me being gay, then say so. Be honest, don't hide behind dogma."

"Yes, okay, I do not understand this life you choose." I frowned. She sighed and handed me the sugar bowl. "No, not choose, are part of because you are born so. God made you gay. He does not make mistakes, so all the gays in the world are perfect examples of God's wonders."

I snickered as I stirred sugar into coffee rugged enough to eat the barnacles off the side of a tugboat.

"You *have* been talking with Elizabeth."

"She has been talking to me and your father and your cousins. She is stubborn like a mule."

"She takes after you," I pointed out.

Mamá shook her head, her freshly painted fingernails tapping on the sides of her mug. "*Sí*, yes, in many ways, as do all of you. But also, you are all your own persons. Juan is a funny man, so happy to be single. I do not understand him or any of my children, but because I do not understand does not mean I should not *try* to understand. So please help me to understand you, Alejandro. When did you know you did not like girls in the normal way?"

I raised an eyebrow, but she didn't get that arched brow. This was going to take time. A lot of time. I glanced at the clock on the wall. I wasn't sure we had enough time to cover this one simple question this morning, but I tried my best to explain how I'd come to realize that I was different than the other guys on my team, in my classrooms, in my family.

"Your *Tía* Celeste was a lesbian," she whispered after my lengthy explanation, as if she were afraid the Virgin would overhear that admission and scowl at her. "I loved her very much but did not see why she would pick to be alone instead of being with a man. This sort of thing, this being out and gay marches through town, didn't happen when I was young, and so it was hidden away. Celeste was asked to move away. She died alone, her *friendly roommate* passing two years before she did. Alejandro, I do not want you to die alone."

I slid my hand across the table, rolled it over, and opened my fingers. She put her hand into mine, and I squeezed her fingers.

"I won't. I have Sebastian. *Mamá*, I'm really mad that you've forbidden him from coming to the party." Her face tightened. "It's simply not fair."

"Alejandro, your friend—"

"Boyfriend. He is my boyfriend."

Her lips flattened a bit. Someone upstairs began singing *Beauty and the Beast* at the top of her lungs. My sister was going to burst into a supernova before the day was done.

"Yes, of course. Your boyfriend is a smart man, calm and older, mature. He sees that right now, at this party, your being gay in front of the family is going to do more harm than good. Sometimes we must pick our battles. Let today be your sister's day."

"I will, but I want you to know that the next time

there's a family event, I'm bringing Sebastian, and I will not hide outside or in a corner."

"I understand." She patted my hand. I truly wasn't sure how much she grasped, but she had been warned. "Now, go let *Tía* Margarita trim your hair."

I passed on the haircut but did give my shoes a polish when the dullness of them was mentioned by several aunts. By ten a.m., the house was packed. By eleven, we were all in transit to Our Lady of Guadalupe Church for the short mass. Elizabeth, my parents, and her royal court entered the church first; the rest of us followed. My sister was in a bright yellow ball gown. She truly did look like a Disney princess, and so did her court. My father had yet to talk to me, as had most of my cousins. Héctor had not shown up, which was wise. After my sister received the sacrament, she placed a live bouquet at the base of the statue of the Virgin and received a new Bible, rosary, and a ring from Father Delgadillo.

Then we were whisked off in rented limos to the Desert Winds Restaurant, just four blocks from our church, for the party. The room my parents had rented was decorated in yellow, white, and gold. The tables all had white cloths, beautiful yellow floral arrangements, and gold flatware to match the gilt-edged china plates. There were roughly two hundred people coming, so the massive room was packed full of round tables, as well as a long table for my sister and her court. With so many eyes on me, I hung back, trying to be as unassuming as possible. That was easy, as my sister Elizabeth was so beautiful that all eyes were on her throughout. No one said anything to me, but plenty was said about me. I saw the odd looks, heard the whispers when I'd pass by.

I stayed through the whole thing. Got to see my father and baby sister dance, and yes, he cried but hid it well. The surprise dance was fun, and the food was delicious, the catering company bringing out tons of rich, spicy Mexican food that was almost as good as my mother's cooking. Almost. The bar was open, the music loud, and my family was in full celebration mode. I made my escape when everyone, including *Abuela*, was on the dance floor. Slipping outside, I paused by the rear exit, drew in some hot air, and let it out slowly. I lingered in the shade for a minute, calling an Uber out for a ride and trying to shrug off the contempt from so many in my family. I really wasn't sure what was worse—the silent looks of disgust or a punch in the face. Not that I'd been punched, but I'd have rather thrown down with a few of my male cousins than be subjected to the revulsion on so many faces. Faces of those I'd played with since I'd been in diapers.

The door opened, slapping me in the ass. I leaped aside to let whatever smoker needed a puff out. My father stepped around the door, his gaze dropping on me. My fingers tightened on my phone. He was so handsome in a suit that was almost the same smoke gray as mine. His hair was combed back, the silver strands pronounced.

"I can go around front to wait for my ride," I offered, seeing the unease working its way into his face.

He stared up at the trees swaying in the wind. "Will you be home for your mother's birthday in August?"

"*Sí papá, si me permiten volver a casa.*"

His dark eyes narrowed in confusion. "Why would you not be allowed to come home? You are our son, no matter what you are. That will never change."

Okay, wow. That was not actual hate, I didn't think. I could deal.

"Thank you. If I come, Sebastian comes with me."

He studied the trees at length. I checked my phone. My ride was a minute away. "I understand," he finally replied, then went back inside.

Well, that was also not a real answer, but again, I could deal. He hadn't slapped me or called me a foul name. I sprinted around the front of the restaurant, pulling my tie free as I ran, and dove into the nice cool backseat of a Honda Accord.

I couldn't get back to Sebastian's loving arms fast enough.

EIGHTEEN

Seb

THE TONE of social media had changed. Not enough to mean I was out of a job, but enough to make me think my strategies were working. I was convinced that if the JAR line stopped making the plays and getting the goals, it wouldn't be so easy for our fans to accept that Alex was gay. They were becoming heroes in the team, along with Colorado, who was getting steadier with each game he played. Today we had the final promo shoot, three games to go in the full season, and we were actually going to secure a fixed fourth place in our eight, even though we had no statistical chance of getting to the Stanley Cup run.

The mood was high, we were hosting San Diego at home, and Jason was talking *at* me about the contribution I'd made for the team.

"… so if we could retain you to back us up on email, that would be great."

He was waiting for an answer, for me to say that it was wonderful that the team put so much faith in what I'd been doing, and that yes, I'd love to carry on working with the Raptors, remotely, from my home office in the UK.

Only I didn't want to say that, because even *considering* part-time distance support meant I was leaving, and about now, I wasn't ready to leave.

"Uh-huh," I offered, and his face fell.

"Of course, I get your other contract work fills your time and that we couldn't pay you for the fixed period, but you added value here, Seb, and we have so much more we need you to work on. We could pay you," he added a little desperately. I knew gate receipts were up, but I wasn't sure they were up *that much*. Hell, it wasn't as if I needed the money, anyway. Still, this was a big decision to make.

"I'll think about it," I said, and then because Jason looked like a kicked puppy, I clapped him on the shoulder. "But I've loved working with the Raptors, so why would I want to stop now?"

That was enough to make my friend smile, and with that done, I was free to escape him and Mark, who had also suggested some long-distance contract work. They both understood my home was England, but what about Alex?

If I went home, we'd maybe see each other a few times a year, a long summer, and that was it. I was the one with the dual passport, so I could be the one who split my time between England and Arizona. Would Alex want that? Was he counting on me just being here for a limited time? Why was I even doubting him? Or me? I loved him, and he loved me.

"Hey."

Talk of the devil. Alex appeared, still in his suit and

tie, heading for the locker rooms and suiting up for the game.

"Hey," I stayed neutral in case my tone gave away things I didn't want it to.

"So I was thinking," Alex said with a frown as he examined my expression.

"Yeah?"

"I want to spend time with Henry over the summer, maybe stay with him some, but you know what? I tracked down a trainer who moved away from the US, set up a place near Oxford, and you know what? I've never been to England."

I turned to face him, not entirely sure I was hearing right.

"Alex?"

"You're going home. I have time. Maybe I could go to England for a few weeks. You can show me—"

"Yes."

He grinned, then winked at me before heading for the lockers. I could delay thinking about what happened after the summer because for a little while, I would have Alex in my house, and that was a hundred kinds of awesome.

"You look like the Cheshire cat," Colorado observed as he passed me. I had nothing to say to that because I was smiling too damn hard.

———

I HAD SO much to show Alex. As soon as we landed, I was telling him things.

"And Windsor Castle isn't that far from here either. We could go if you want to?" I think that was about the tenth thing I'd suggested to him in the space of a few minutes, and he looked at me with wide eyes and mouth open.

"Is that before the place where King thingy married Princess whatever, or Stonehenge or not Stonehenge because it's too commercial, or Bath where the Romans were, or is it after the whole City of London tour?"

He was teasing me, I knew that, and I felt the heat in my face. I couldn't help it. I wanted to tell him everything about my home. History was everywhere around me, and I'd just assumed those were the things an American new to the country would want to see.

He laughed then and placed a hand on my knee. "I'm messing with you. I want to see it all, but most of all, I want to meet your mom and see your house, so can we do that first?"

"We can do that." I took the exit onto the motorway and headed northwest, away from London and out to the Cotswolds, and we settled into our journey as if we'd driven together forever. There was music, teasing, and just short of two hours later, we pulled up outside my place.

"Oh wow," Alex said and clambered out of the car. I wondered what he saw when he looked at the yellowed stone building, the middle of three former workers' cottages, complete with slate roof and roses climbing around the front door. I loved my house, my security, and that my mom and aunt lived next door was just an added benefit. Could I leave this? A pang hit me as I even touched on the idea.

"It's like out of a film." Alex shook his head. "It's beautiful."

"It was built in the 1700s—"

He kissed me, right in front of my house, behind the rose bushes, and I held him close.

"Thank you for bringing me. I love it. Will I hit my head in there? Are there beams? Is there an open fire? Can we have a fire?" He added the last part with a dubious tone. "I guess that's only for winter, right? Which house is your mom's? Can we meet her?"

"Yes, you will hit your head, no to the fire, and come with me." I took his hand and tugged him down the path and up to the front door of my mum's place. I didn't have to knock, and I knew my mum and aunt would have been waiting for us.

"Sebastian!" Mum shouted as she opened the door, pulling me close and holding me tight. This woman had sacrificed everything for me, and I loved her for everything, and so I hugged her just as hard. When we parted, she immediately gathered Alex in for a hug. All I could think was that my mum at just over five foot was tiny compared to my boyfriend. "You must be Alex. Come in, come in, welcome to England. Sebastian tells me that you play hockey, on a team in the desert. How does that even work?" I listened to their voices fade as they headed for the kitchen, and then my aunt Olivia was hugging me and telling me how much they'd missed me.

"I missed you all too," I agreed with feeling and allowed myself to be led into the kitchen, where they'd outdone themselves with food. "Your mum said we didn't have enough, but we can always get more."

"A scone?" I heard Alex ask, he and my mum bent over the kitchen table, which seemed to be in danger of collapsing under the weight of food.

"That's right, and we put jam and cream on it, clotted cream mind you."

"Clotted? Okay, you'd better show me how. This is the jam, right? Jelly, you mean, which goes first?"

"Mum, you need to let us get in the house before you try to feed him."

Mum glanced up at me. "Oh, sweetheart, Alex is adorable, and he tells me that he's going to show me hockey, and we're going shopping."

How the hell had all that happened in the space of a minute? God knows, but my mum was fast.

"Aunt Olivia, this is my boyfriend, Alex." Olivia and Alex hugged, Mum and I hugged again, Alex and I hugged. Hell, we were all hugging so long that I thought we'd never sit down. When we eventually took our seats, I watched Mum show Alex how to build the perfect scone for his cream tea, explain what Battenberg cake was, and how to make a good cup of tea, and through all of this, Alex was smiling, and it didn't even dim when Aunt Olivia pinched his cheek, then patted his head. He was so happy here, and I wanted to keep him in this kitchen forever.

When we'd eaten and promised to pick both ladies up in the morning for a day visiting Roman ruins— Alex's choice—we headed for my place. I cleared hanging space for him, and we unpacked our cases from the bed. "Just put everything of yours on the left of the wardrobe." I pointed at it just in case.

"Closet." Alex smirked.

I picked up a pair of his jeans. "Yep, put your trousers in the wardrobe."

He moved closer and took the jeans off me, then

tossed them onto my chair. "You want me to put my pants in the closet?"

"Yeah, trousers—" He kissed me to stop me from talking, linked his hands behind my neck, and then broke the kiss.

"Say something else," he ordered. "You get me so hot."

"About my wardrobe?" I smirked into the kiss.

"And sidewalks, tell me all that again." He pressed himself against me, and while I'd never thought my English accent was particularly sexy, I mean it was just the way I talked, it seemed to be having an effect on Alex, who was hard against me. I guided him to the bed until the back of his legs hit it, and then I went full-out Brit.

"Later I'm going to take you out for a stroll on your holiday, along the pavement, and find fish and chips from a takeaway, and then when we're done, I'm going to bring you back, and after you've used the loo, we're going hang your trousers in the wardrobe, close the curtains, turn off all the lights, and then use a torch to find—"

I didn't get any further with my ridiculous Brit-speak story as he yanked me onto the bed, bags pushed off onto the floor, and he showed me just how much my talking had turned him on.

I'd never been happier to be British.

WE HAD four weeks and toured around the countryside, just being in love. Work waited, and apart from a couple of hours here and there, I had my first real break since university. I introduced Alex to the awesome that was an

English country pub, we went over the border into Wales and spent a long, hot, sexy weekend in Cardiff, and we visited so many places that I hadn't seen myself. Sometimes we held hands when no one could see us, but the paranoid part of me thought that one photo was all it took to get back to the US. Who would recognize Alex here I didn't know, but one Raptors fan holidaying here, and his secret was toast. We never talked seriously, not until it was two days until Alex's flight home and he'd been growing progressively quieter and more thoughtful. I carefully avoided any mention of his impending return to the States, letting him set the agenda, but so far, he'd stayed very quiet about anything like a future.

We'd gone for a walk along the river that ran through the small town of Bourton-on-the-Water, crossing each of the five bridges as we talked about hockey and us, but by the time we arrived back, it wasn't as if we'd come to any kind of resolution over what came next.

I sensed that Alex had something to say but wouldn't say it, and my heart was scared for what he might say, so I found myself changing the subject whenever we got serious.

I know that I wanted to offer everything but didn't want to overwhelm him and force something on him that wasn't right for him.

Like this, we were at a miserable impasse. Reaching the house, he paused at the gate, and instead of pushing it open, he turned to me, and I sensed this was the moment everything in my head, all my fears and worries, would come true.

"I've always wanted to play hockey," he blurted.

"I know. You've said that before." I was cautious and

didn't think it was wise to ask him why he was telling me this.

"But I could be a tour guide, in Bath or Cardiff. I could learn it all and stay here with you. I could give it up for you if you asked me to."

My chest tightened. This wasn't what he wanted, not really.

"Let's go inside," I encouraged, and somehow we made it inside and shut the front door behind us. "That's not what you want," I said when he just stared at me as if he was in shock. "Your family means so much to you, and I couldn't accept you giving up hockey, for goodness sake. The ice is your home, and you come alive out there."

"I don't want this to end," he said, almost desperate.

"Maybe it's run its course," I suggested. "You need to go out there and see what else you can have. You don't have to settle for the first man you fall for."

He slumped into the nearest chair and hunched his shoulders. "Is that what you think? I can't believe you really believe that. I love you."

"And I love you." I took the chair opposite.

"Then why are you pushing me away?"

"I'm not, Alex."

"You won't talk about us seeing each other again."

"I was waiting for you to start the conversation."

"And I was waiting for you."

We were talking in circles, but one thing was clear—we were both avoiding the elephant in the corner.

"Alex, talk to me."

"Come back to America with me. I mean, you wouldn't have to live there, but you said your dad was American, so you could get a passport if you wanted."

"I already have one."

"Oh." His eyes widened. "*Oh*," he repeated.

"That doesn't mean I want to leave England."

"I know that you wouldn't want to move to the US, but what if I could get a place a bit farther away from the arena. You could stay for longer periods of time, maybe even a few months in the winter? I'm sure there are plenty of contracts and places that need your help. Even if you came back a couple of times, we could Skype other times…" I knew he was waiting for me to say something. I moved to sit next to him.

"I love you," I began.

"Shit, you're going to give me a but, aren't you," he murmured.

"The but…" I sighed. "Alex, I'm the first guy who you've been with, and you should—"

"You want me to go out and fuck some guys? Huh?"

I winced at the crude word. What we did wasn't fucking. We made love. What we had was real and special.

"No."

"You're so experienced at thirty-freaking-two," he snapped. "Is that what you did, fucked your way around England?"

Mostly, I'd spent all hours I was given working to get my consultancy off the ground, but yeah, I'd done my share of shitty relationships, only none of them were like this. I'd never fallen in love before, and who was to say whether falling in love at twenty-two or thirty-two was the right way of doing things.

"No, and we don't fuck. We make love. There's a difference. If I thought for one minute…"

"What?" he prompted. "What do you think? Seb, talk to me?"

"If I thought that you were truly ready for the kind of forever I want with you, if I didn't feel as if I was making you commit to me—"

He was getting way too good at shutting me up with kisses, but I stopped him. "Alex—"

"I want forever. With you. And one day I want to come out and be an inspiration to hockey kids and buy a place together and have you be there sometimes when you can. Bring your mom out and your aunt. When I get the big contract, I can pay for it all, and Christ, Seb, I love you so much I can't bear the thought of this being it." His tone was exasperated, desperate, and then he just sounded overwhelmed. "What do I have to say to make you see—?"

This time I shut him up with a kiss, and then I pulled back. "I love you. Let's make this work."

"Together, in the US, here, your mom visiting, the house, you want everything?"

Now that was an easy question to answer.

"I want everything. With you."

Epilogue

ALEX

"LIFT YOUR LEG HIGHER. Yeah, that's... yeah."

He writhed under me, his body tightening around me as I went deeper.

"Ah hell," Sebastian crooned, his fingers tugging the fitted sheet free as I bumped his prostate over and over.

His back was slick with sweat, stuck to my chest, his face resting on the bared mattress. I loved this so much. The hard male body under me, the masculine grunts, the way his ass felt, the heat and pressure. This was my world, my man, my whole being, all swaddled up in this massive bed in a lovely Cotswold home.

"Do that again... no, yes." He arched his back, and the sensation nearly made my head blow off my shoulders. The pleasure of being inside him was unexplainable. No words could ever do it justice. Sebastian was such a giving teacher, and I was an eager student. We'd not worked up to me bottoming yet, but neither of us were in a hurry. Seb loved it, and I was nervous, still, after all this time. Some habits were hard to break.

"Faster, please." His heated words pulled me from the thoughts of an Alejandro who didn't exist anymore, or so I liked to think. Obviously he did. He'd pop up from time to time, berate and judge me, call me sinful and dirty, but then Seb would be there to steer me out of the dark past and into this brilliant present. I spread myself over him, wiggling his legs even farther apart, my hips pumping.

He angled up to meet my thrusts. I came first, him just a second behind me, his soft cries of completion floating up to the ceiling to join mine. I was shuddering and slick. Then my elbows folded. I fell on his back, enjoying the shivers as he pumped his load into the sheets and his hand.

"Ah, bloody hell," he gasped, rolling his hips round and round, milking his cock.

I licked the nape of his neck, pushed deep one last time, and then pulled out, my feet hitting the floor. Sebastian moved to his back. I could feel his gaze on me as I padded to the bathroom. I tied and tossed the condom into the trash before stepping into the shower. We had a plane to catch today. Our summer in England was over. It was back to Arizona, the Raptors, and my family. Communication between me and ninety percent of the Santos-Garcia clan had been spotty. I spoke daily to my siblings and *Abuela*. My mother weekly, my father not at all, but he wasn't a fan of social media. Mom asked for pictures but never commented on the ones with me and Seb together. Which was kind of hurtful, but at least she was talking to me. My cousins? Not so much. Some of that was on me, but a lot of that gap was on them. I'd pulled away from America the best I could during our time here. I needed to learn how to be a gay man in a committed relationship. I needed to find myself and my spirituality. I needed to be free from the racial tensions. I just needed to *be*. I'd found great peace here in this picturesque village. The people were delightful, the food to die for, and the TV above par. And then there was Sebastian.

Who was, I noted after leaving the shower with a towel around my neck, sound asleep with a contented smile on his lips. I covered his pale ass up, pulled on some comfortable travel clothes, and went to the kitchen to put the kettle on. Tea was the norm now. I missed coffee, especially the sweet Mexican coffee *Mamá* brewed every morning. The instant stuff they sold here was disgusting, so I'd made the switch to tea. As the kettle chugged and steamed, I went to the wide bay window in the corner nook and gazed at the back yard, or garden as Seb called it. See, to me, a garden is a small plot where you grow vegetables. I smiled at the gentle prodding I'd taken over here the past few weeks, all good-natured teasing from Seb, his mom, aunt, and the neighbors about my silly way of speaking or telling time.

"You look a world away," Seb said as he walked up behind me on bare feet. I leaned back into his arms, turning my head for a soft kiss.

"I'm not sure I want to leave here," I confessed, reaching up to push my fingers into his damp hair. He smelled shower fresh. I let my gaze move from him back to the yard as my body settled into his embrace. "We have a birthday party to attend in two days."

"I know." He spoke into the side of my neck. "I'll be there with you."

"If they act badly, we're leaving and never going back."

"Don't make vows that you may wish you'd not made later. They're coming around."

"Hmm." That was all I was going to say about that. Coming around yes, maybe. We'd see at my mother's birthday party. For now, I wanted to simply linger in his arms and enjoy the sun warming the green lawns of the town I now considered my second home. "Can we come back here every summer?"

"If you so wish it, then it shall be so," he teased, nipping my earlobe while hugging me just a bit more tightly. Oh yes, I wished it. I wished it and many other things, but for now, summers in the Cotswolds, winters in Tucson, and watching the day begin in this man's arms was more than enough.

ARIZONA WAS JUST AS HOT, dry, and dusty as it had ever been. Breathing in that air made my restless soul feel a bit more settled. My house was still empty. Ryker was flatly refusing to leave his man and that Minnesota farm until the last whistle blew. He had about ten days. We were at the end of August, and training camp was set to begin September ninth. Sebastian and I had gone round and round all summer about living arrangements. Well, I'd gone round. He'd been his usual properly cool British self, saying that whatever I wished would be. Tut-tut and cheerios and pass the digestives, which was no help at all.

I was still wavering. Moving in with him would be a loud statement, one that I wasn't sure I was ready to make. My family situation was still ugly, so perhaps just sitting still and sharing this house with Ryker and Henry, who was to be discharged in three weeks, might be the most practical thing. Or would it? Ugh.

I gave Seb, seated beside me, a long look after I'd pulled off halfway to San Luis for gas. "I think I should live with Ryker and Henry."

"Okay." He unbuckled his belt, slid out of the Jeep, stretched, and went inside the Gas & Go-Go. I pumped gas, my sight on the roadrunner staring at me from the edge of the highway.

"Beep-beep," I called to the bird. It just stood there, staring. "Okay, so is this some sort of *Mayans MC* thing where an animal appears and has some significant meaning to the episode?" The bird blinked birdy eyes at me. "Like, am I going to run into a wall that some stupid coyote painted to look like a tunnel? Is an Acme anvil going to fall on my head?"

"Are you conversing with that bird?" Seb asked, appearing at my side with two cold cans of soda and a bag of Limón chips. I'd turned him onto those, and the man was addicted to them.

"It's a roadrunner." I placed the nozzle back in the holder and turned to fasten my gas cap tightly.

"Ah, beep-beep and all that." He smiled at me, the wind pushing his hair off his brow.

"I love you. I think I should move in with you."

"Okay." He gave me a quick peck on the cheek, then climbed in and buckled his belt. I rolled my eyes so hard it hurt.

"Why are you not giving me any advice on where to live?" I asked when I climbed back into my Jeep. He'd already opened the bag of chips and was munching on them.

"Well." He paused to wipe his salty fingers on a wad

of napkins crammed under his leg. "It's not my place to make major life decisions for you. Chip?" He held the bag out to me. I shoved my hand in, grumbling, grabbed a bunch, and crammed them into my mouth. "Also, for your information, I got a text from an Adler Lockhart asking me if I knew of any homes for sale near Henry's rehab center. Dare I ask who Adler Lockhart is?"

"Really? Wow, um, he's one of the Railers. Richer than sin. Why is he buying Henry a house when he has one we're all sharing?"

"Seems Henry's leg wasn't healing as they'd wished, so they're going back in to do another surgery, pins and grafts and such, nasty by the sounds. So he cannot live in a house with steps, which yours has. Also, there is some worry about his eye. His vision isn't returning as quickly as it should be so…"

"Damn it. I wish I would have had ten minutes alone with Aarni. *Ese hijueputa con cara de rata!*"

"I understood rat and son of a bitch," Seb stated, handing me a cold drink.

"Yeah, that's all you need to understand to get the gist. So, if Henry's not staying with us, who will take care of him?" This turn of events sucked.

"Well, until Lockhart can secure a housekeeper/cook/personal assistant, it will be Henry's mother," he replied, lifting his chin in the direction of the road. "We should pull away. There's a car behind us."

I threw the guy waiting on my bumper a fast look and a mouthed "Sorry!" before I started the engine. When I hit the highway, the roadrunner was gone. I hoped he didn't run into any suspicious mounds of birdseed.

"That's not going to be cool. Henry said he and his folks don't always get along." I set the cruise control and leaned back, the wind whipping my face as Romeo Santos serenaded us.

"Life is seldom fair," he reminded me gently. True enough.

The ride home was spent trying to teach Sebastian how to greet my mother and father in Spanish, eating chips, and drinking soda that made us both belch. We'd not even pulled up and parked outside my parents' home when Elizabeth ran out of the side door and threw herself at me. Laughing madly, I held her close and swung her in a wide circle, her joyous laughs music to my ears. When her tiny bare feet touched the sidewalk, she was off again, pulling on Sebastian and me until we were tripping over our own feet into the kitchen. There sat my grandmother, my parents, and Dwayne, the young man who my sister had been dating since he had served as her main *chambelán*.

My gaze skittered from *Abuela* smiling at us to my parents. We lingered in the doorway, my hand seeking his and finding it. I jerked my chin up. My father stood. Our sights locked.

"*Bienvenido a casa, hijo.*" He offered me his hand. I shook it. Then he extended his hand to Sebastian. "Welcome back. Thank you for taking care of our son overseas."

"*Gracias por invitarme a su fiesta, es un placer verlo de nuevo,*" Sebastian said, his gaze going from my father to my mother, then to my grandmother.

My grandmother reached up to pinch me on the butt. I snickered, bent down, and pressed a kiss to her weathered cheek.

"I missed you, *Abuela.*"

"*El amor te queda, mi niño,*" she whispered as Dwayne rose and joined Elizabeth in the search for more kitchen chairs. I stared over my mother's head as she fell into a conversation about the royals with Sebastian. He gave me a sly wink on the side when she asked if he knew Prince Harry, whom she liked a great deal since he had married an American woman of color.

Yeah, I guess love maybe did look good on me, hard to say, but I did know that it felt great. As did sitting at this table with Sebastian at my side. Maybe I would move in with him after all. Time would tell. One thing was for sure. No matter where our mail went, our hearts were forever joined.

The End

Next for the Raptors

Shadows and Light (Raptors #3)

Is it easier to fall into the shadows than hold on to the light?

Injured in a horrific car accident by a man who made him feel like nothing, Henry was left with life-threatening injuries, his career as a hockey player on hold, and nightmares that chase him in his sleep. He's struggling to walk, and as much as people tell him to have hope because he's young and fit, his vision is compromised, and he's spiraling into despair. He's finally been allowed home to the house he shares with Ryker and Alex, but his mom is caring for him, and her resolution that he will never see a rink again is driving him insane. She wants him to move home and join the family's realty company, but the thought of that is terrifying. Hockey gave him freedom, and now it's all been taken away.

Drugs work to take the edge off, but it's only risky

experimental surgery that will fix his eye. On the one hand, if the invasive operation is successful, he could one day get back on the ice, but on the other, if it fails, he could be left permanently blind. Sending his mom away gives Henry back the illusion of control, but loneliness kills him one day at a time until Apollo arrives at his house and tells him that they're moving. With his sunny smile and infectious optimism, along with his no-nonsense rules, Apollo slowly becomes an integral part of Henry's life. But one day, when Henry is better, Apollo will leave, and what happens then? Has Henry really fallen for the dark-eyed man, or is it all just smoke and mirrors?

If there is one thing that Apollo Vasquez knows all about, it's helping others and living with quirky athletes. After all, he's spent most of his adult life tending to one of the richest hockey-playing heirs in America. His days have been filled with friendship, laughter, and the knowledge that he's needed. Or he used to be. Over the past year, Apollo's best friend, Adler Lockhart, has been slipping away, his time spent with his boyfriend, on the ice, or traveling the world with the man he loves. This leaves Apollo feeling like a clunky third wheel or all alone in a luxurious apartment with no one to fuss over.

Knowing that his life is at a crossroads, his loving nature leads him far away from his childhood friend to the dry desert town of Tucson, where he signs on to care for Henry Greenaway as the young Raptor recovers both mentally and physically from a near-fatal car crash. Henry is also facing a new life, one that might lead him from the sport he has loved for so long. Cooking, cleaning, and providing moral support is just what the doctor ordered for Apollo, and he soon finds that he's not only rediscovering himself and a new life he adores but also falling for the sweet, lost, injured man who's slowly capturing his heart one timid smile at a time.

Shadow and Light

Hockey Series' from RJ Scott & V.L. Locey

Harrisburg Railers

Owatonna U Hockey

Arizona Raptors

Boston Rebels

LA Storm

Chesterford Coyotes - Young Adult

When hockey wunderkind Tennant Rowe meets his new coach, he knows he's in trouble. Jared Madsen is nine years older than Tennant, impossibly attractive, and — worst of all — his brother's off-limits best friend. Is their chemistry worth the risk?

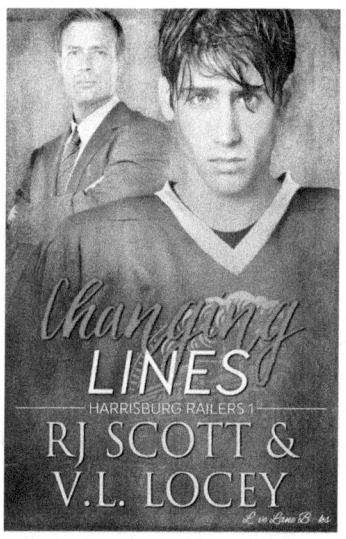

Changing Lines (Railers 1)

Can Tennant show Jared that age is just a number, and that love is all that matters?

The Rowe Brothers are famous hockey hotshots, but as the youngest of the trio, Tennant has always had to play against his brothers' reputations. To get out of their shadows, and against their advice, he accepts a trade to the Harrisburg Railers, where he runs into Jared Madsen. Mads is an old family friend and his brother's one-time teammate. Mads is Tennant's new coach. And Mads is the sexiest thing he's ever laid eyes on.

Jared Madsen's hockey career was cut short by a fault in his heart, but coaching keeps him close to the game. When Ten is traded to the team, his carefully organized world is thrown into chaos. Nine years his junior and his best friend's brother, he knows Ten is strictly off-limits, but as soon as he sees Ten's moves, on and off the ice, he knows that his heart could get him into trouble again.

Changing Lines

Harrisburg Railers (Hockey Romance)

Railers Volume 1 | Railers Volume 2 | Railers Volume 3 | Railers Volume 4

Meet the men of Owatonna University's hockey team

Ryker (Owatonna U, 1)

Ryker

Ryker is hockey royalty, Jacob is a poor country boy. Can two vastly different people find common ground and become the men they want to be?

Ryker comes from a long line of championship-winning hockey players. Playing college hockey to develop his game is his only focus, and nothing will stand in the way of him working to become the best player. He has no room for relationships, people who point out his flaws, or anyone who calls him on his dreams. He certainly has no place for love, and meeting Jacob is nothing but a useful distraction on the side. After all trying to get his Owatonna Eagles teammate into bed is less work and more play. When tragedy rocks his family, his charmed life crumbles, and the only person he can turn to is the same one who claims to hate him.

Jacob Benson has only known hard work and stifling conservative values his whole life. Born and raised in the small rural community of Eden Crossing, Minnesota, he's the only son of a hard-working but struggling dairy farming family. Jacob is using his skills in hockey to finance his way to an agricultural science degree. These four years at Owatonna U. will probably be the only time he has to enjoy life, gain acceptance about his sexuality, and live openly before his inevitable return to the farm. Running into a pretty rich boy like Ryker Madsen is putting a damper on his enjoyment of life away from home. Ryker's flip, conceited, carefree attitude grates on Jacob's every nerve. So why, if Ryker is everything he dislikes, does he want nothing more than to explore the sinful dreams that his annoying teammate stars in every night?

Ryker

Owatonna U Hockey (Hockey Romance)

1. Ryker
2. Scott
3. Benoit
4. Christmas Lights
5. Valentine's Hearts
6. Desert Dreams

Coast to Coast (Arizona Raptors 1)

Coast To Coast

When opposites attract, this bottom-of-the-league team will never be the same again.

A stipulation in his father's will forces Mark back into the arms of a family that disowned him and leaves him one-third owner of a hockey team facing financial ruin. He doesn't even watch hockey, let alone like it, and wants nothing more than to head back to New York. Then there's the new coach, a stubborn, opinionated, irritating man with superiority issues and questionable music taste. Butting heads with Rowen becomes the new normal, but it comes with passionate debate and an all-consuming lust.

Challenged to rebuild one of the worst teams in the league into a future cup contender, Rowen can't pass up the opportunity. Never in his twenty years of hockey has he ever seen a team managed so badly or coached players overflowing with resentment and bigotry. Yet there's something about this team and this city that compels him to roll up his sleeves and start dismantling. If only Mark, one of three siblings who now own the Raptors, wasn't so damned rock-headed yet so damned appealing his job might be easier. It doesn't look like either is willing to give in, but one night in a dark, desert hotel changes everything.

Coast To Coast

Arizona Raptors (Hockey Romance)

1. Coast To Coast
2. Across the Pond
3. Shadow and Light
4. Sugar and Ice
5. School and Rock

Top Shelf (Boston Rebels 1)

Top Shelf

Acting on the attraction to his best friend's brother has always been off the table for Xander until a passionate hookup with Mason at a beach resort begins a love affair that burns long after summer ends.

Mason specializes in assisting same-sex couples on their journey to becoming parents and fighting every rule that blocks his way in the stuck-in-the-past agency that hired him. Living in his brother's pool house is rent-free, and every cent he earns he saves for his dream—that one day he'd have his own company helping others. The downside is that he has to see his annoying brother every day, the upside is that his brother's teammates from the Boston Rebels make regular visits. The eye candy that passes Mason's window is almost enough to make him consider dating a hockey player, but not just any player though. Ever since Xander—his brother's childhood friend—came out as gay at a press conference, Mason's puppy love has turned into a burning attraction he can no longer ignore.

Hockey has been one of Xander's main focuses since he was old enough to balance on skates. Well, hockey and Mason Kingsley, but Mason was always unattainable. Now that he's about to see thirty candles on his birthday cake and is no longer hiding the fact he's gay, he's ready to find a soul mate to make his life complete. A summer vacation is just what he needs to have time to think, but when the Boston Rebels arriving in paradise with Mason in tow, thinking is the last thing he needs. One torrid night under a balmy moon and rules about not messing with his best friend's brother vanish on a warm, tropical breeze.

Summer romances don't generally last past Labor Day, but with the new season about to begin Xander and Mason are going to have to face the world and decide if their love is real enough to withstand everything.

Top Shelf

Boston Rebels

Lost In Boston (Free Prequel Novella)

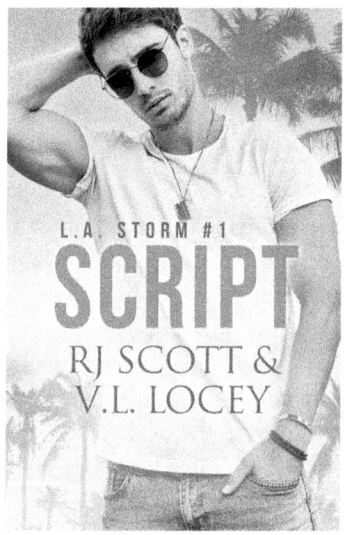

Script (LA Storm, 1)

Script

Hollywood A-lister Finn might be Canadian, but he needs Cameron to show him how to hockey.

Actor Finn Kerrigan is at a crossroads. After growing up a soap star, then starring in a hugely successful trilogy of action movies, he's finally given the chance to read a heartfelt and passionate script that could change his life forever. The role would be enough for people to see him as a serious actor, and maybe even win him an award or two (and no, a golden raspberry award for his action movies doesn't count). Once established as a serious actor he's sure he can come out of the closet and finally live his truth. When he lies to get the part of a hockey player on a struggling team, he suddenly has nowhere to hide. He might be Canadian, but the last time he skated he was ten, and no, he doesn't have hockey in his blood. With only a month until filming starts, he about to be exposed, but partnered with a player who's supposed to be giving him tips, he doesn't realize how many of his secrets will come to light. Falling in lust, one heated kiss at a time, is inevitable, but giving Cameron up at the end of the shoot could break his heart.

Cameron Chavkin is the face of the LA Storm. And the body, and the hair, and the smile. He's at the prime of his career, men and women want to be with him, and he's skating better than he ever has before. His house sits next to a famous rock star's mansion, his garage is filled with expensive cars, and he's even been asked to mentor a once-famous actor in a new hockey movie. Life is pretty sweet. Until the bad boy of hockey meets Finn, a man on the edge with more secrets than Cameron has endorsements. Knowing better than to get involved, Cameron is swept up despite himself, and when it's time to say goodbye to the Storm's most eligible bachelor is finding it hard to follow the script.

Script

LA Storm

1. Script
2. Second
3. *Shield*
4. *Spiral*

Off The Ice (Chesterford Coyotes, 1)

Off The Ice

A coming-of-age love story with high school, hockey rivalry, friendship, family, and coming out.

Soren's life changes in an instant when he and his younger brother are adopted by hockey royalty. Making sense of his new life is hard enough, but when he's enrolled in a private school it means facing a whole new set of problems. Navigating friendship, family, and hockey is one thing, but being attracted to the boy who vexes him is a whole new thing.

Felix has a reputation to protect. He's the kid who seems to have everything but looks can be deceiving. Spinning lies about his perfect life, he's created a fantasy world that even he has started to believe. Only, it's not long before everything crumbles, all of his pretty lies are revealed, and only his closest rival sees through his pain and stands by him.

Fighting is easy, friendship is hard, but love is everything.

Off The Ice

Chesterford Coyotes

1. Off The Ice
2. On Thin Ice
3. *Dance on Ice*

Also By RJ Scott

For a full list of ebooks and links please scan the code above or
visit rjscott.co.uk/rjbooks

Meet RJ Scott

RJ discovered romance in books at a very young age and realized that if there wasn't romance on the page, she could create it in her head. With over one hundred and fifty books published, she is a full time author of gay romance.

She lives and works out of her home in the beautiful English countryside, spends her spare time reading, watching films, and enjoying time with her family.

The last time she had a week's break from writing she didn't like it one little bit and has yet to meet a box of chocolates she couldn't defeat.

www.rjscott.co.uk | rj@rjscott.co.uk

NEWSLETTER - rjscott.co.uk/rjnews

facebook.com/author.rjscott

x.com/Rjscott_author

instagram.com/rjscott_author

amazon.com/author/rj-scott

bookbub.com/authors/rj-scott

goodreads.com/rjscott

pinterest.com/rjscottauthor

Also By VL Locey

For a full list of ebooks and links please scan the code above or
visit vllocey.com/stories-from-vl-locey

Meet V.L. Locey

V.L. Locey loves worn jeans, yoga, belly laughs, walking, reading and writing lusty tales, Greek mythology, the New York Rangers, comic books, and coffee.

(Not necessarily in that order.)

She shares her life with her husband, her daughter, one dog, two cats, a flock of assorted domestic fowl, and two Jersey steers.

When not writing spicy romances, she enjoys spending her day with her menagerie in the rolling hills of Pennsylvania with a cup of fresh java in hand.

vllocey.com
vicki@vllocey.com

Newsletter - vllocey.com/newsletter

facebook.com/V.L.Locey

x.com/vllocey

instagram.com/vl_locey

bookbub.com/authors/v-l-locey

goodreads.com/vllocey

pinterest.com/vllocey